HOW I SURVIVED MIDDLE SCHOOL

Wish Upon a Star

Check out these other books in the
How I Survived Middle School series by Nancy Krulik:

HOW I SURVIVED MIDDLE SCHOOL

Wish Upon a Star

By Nancy Krulik

SCHOLASTIC INC.

New York   Toronto   London   Auckland
Sydney   Mexico City   New Delhi   Hong Kong

For Danny, the musician *I've* had a crush on for years.

ISBN-13: 978-0-545-13270-1
ISBN-10: 0-545-13270-3

12 11 10 9 8 7 6 5 4   10 11 12 13 14/0

Printed in the U.S.A.
First printing, December 2009

Do You Dare?

TRUTH OR DARE: Are you the kind of girl who plays it safe, or do you venture off into the unknown every chance you get? Find out just how much of a wild child is hiding inside you. Take this quiz. We dare you!

1. **You're at a restaurant with your best friends. You scan the menu for a while, and then the waiter appears to take your order. What do you do?**

   A. Try something new and different, as long as it's made with chicken.

   B. Find the most exotic thing on the menu — even if it's snails — and go with that.

   C. Order spaghetti and meatballs. It's hard for anyone to mess that up.

2. **Woohoo! You and your BFF have just arrived at the amusement park. Which ride do you want to hit first?**

   A. The new, super-deluxe roller coaster. It makes two 360-degree loops!

   B. The merry-go-round. Hey, you're feeling nostalgic.

   C. The Ferris wheel. You hear the view from the top is amazing.

3. It's Career Day at school. Which job do you find yourself the most drawn to?

A. Teacher
B. FBI agent
C. Accountant

4. Your history teacher has assigned everyone an oral report to present to the class. You've done all your research and your note cards are prepared. But how do you react when it's time to actually give your report to the class?

A. You volunteer to go third. At least then you'll get it over with pretty quickly.
B. You raise your hand high and volunteer to go first. You love talking to a captive audience.
C. You sink down low in your chair and hope the teacher forgets to call on you.

5. You're looking for the perfect outfit for the school dance. Where do you go to shop?

A. A department store. They make it so easy — you can just buy exactly what's on the mannequin and your whole outfit is good to go.

B. A thrift store — you'll find all sorts of interesting vintage pieces that you can put together for your look.

C. The new boutique in town. You know you'll look really cool in a funky designer dress.

6. Your friend has scored an invite to the hottest party in town, and she's asked you to go. The only catch is, she's the only person you'll know there and she might be a little late. What do you do?

A. Tell her you don't mind going late — you'll meet at her house and walk over together.

B. Wait for her on the corner outside the party so you can go in together.

C. Meet her at the party — you don't want to miss a minute of the fun. Besides, you're sure you'll find someone to talk to.

7. Cute boy alert! The guy you've been crushing on is standing right in front of you in the food line in the cafeteria. What's your plan of action?

A. Smile brightly and ask him if he thinks the sloppy joes are any good today.

B. Keep quiet. You don't want to make a fool of yourself by saying something stupid.

C. Reach past him for a cup of soup, and flash him a dazzling grin.

8. **It's a snow day! Everyone you know has gathered at the big hill behind the school for a day of sledding. Suddenly you spot the cute guy from your biology class at the top of the slope. What do you do?**

A. Start building a snowman at the bottom of the hill — you don't want to risk falling off your sled right in front of him.

B. Sled down the hill — if you tip over, maybe he'll come over and rescue you.

C. Ask him if he wants to sled down the hill with you.

Now it's time to add up your score:

1.	A. 2 points	B. 3 points	C. 1 point
2.	A. 3 points	B. 1 point	C. 2 points
3.	A. 2 points	B. 3 points	C. 1 point
4.	A. 2 points	B. 3 points	C. 1 point
5.	A. 1 point	B. 3 points	C. 2 points
6.	A. 1 point	B. 2 points	C. 3 points
7.	A. 3 points	B. 1 point	C. 2 points
8.	A. 1 point	B. 2 points	C. 3 points

What does your score say about you?

18-24 points: One thing is for sure — you are BORN TO BE WILD! There's nothing you won't say or do. That definitely keeps life exciting. Still, it doesn't hurt to look before you leap every once in a while.

13-17 points: You're the kind of girl who knows when to take a risk and when to play it safe. That means you can have fun without worrying about getting yourself into trouble. Bravo!

8-12 points: You avoid risks at all costs. That may keep you out of the danger zone, but you might be missing out on some good times as well. No one says you should start skydiving, but you might want to try putting yourself out there a little more. Introducing yourself to a new person or trying out a new fashion look could be fun.

Chapter
ONE

*"She said, my rule is no kisses on the first date.
I said, I don't follow rules, this is fate!"*

I tried not to giggle as my friend Chloe danced around her room singing along with the new song by our favorite singer, Cody Tucker. It wasn't easy to keep from laughing — Chloe looked pretty funny as she leaped up and down and twirled around and around. But when she plopped down on her bed and planted a long kiss on her pillow, I couldn't hold it in anymore. I burst out laughing.

"What?" Chloe asked me. She sounded annoyed. "That's what the whole song is about. Cody Tucker kissing his girlfriend."

"I know," I said, trying — unsuccessfully — to stop laughing. "But, Chloe, that's your *pillow*."

"Don't you have any imagination?" Chloe demanded. "I'm *pretending* this is Cody. It's as close as I'll ever get to him."

I sighed. Apparently my imagination wasn't as vivid as Chloe's. To me, her pillow just looked like her pillow.

Still, I knew what she meant. Everyone I knew was dying to meet Cody Tucker. He was the cutest, most talented singer ever!

I wondered how many other girls at Joyce Kilmer Middle School kissed their pillows, pretending they were kissing Cody Tucker. There were probably a lot more than anyone would think. It was just that most of those girls would never do it in front of anyone else. But Chloe knew I would never tell anyone about the whole pillow-kissing thing. That's the kind of friendship Chloe and I have. We keep each other's secrets.

Not that it was any secret that Chloe loved Cody Tucker. He was all she talked about these days. It was "Did you know Cody Tucker's mom was once a dance teacher?" or "Have you heard that Cody Tucker wasn't very good in math when he was in middle school?" all day long.

"Hey, Jenny," Chloe said as the song ended. "Did you know that Cody Tucker's favorite season is summer? That's the same as mine. I'm telling you, Cody and I are meant for each other."

I laughed. "Chloe, Cody Tucker is a big star, and an adult. You're still in middle school. What could you two possibly have in common — other than loving summer, I mean?"

"Well, for one thing, we both hate math. And for another, I'm going to be a big star someday, just like Cody," Chloe replied, as though she was stating a well-known fact, not something she was really hoping for. "I'm already on screens all over town."

I knew what Chloe meant. She was talking about *Webcast Underground*, a computer webcast my friends and I did once a week. But being on a middle school webcast wasn't the same as being an international singing sensation like Cody Tucker.

Still, there wasn't any point in telling Chloe that. Deep down, I had a feeling she already knew it. She just wasn't about to admit it. So instead I said, "I think we should start studying for the Spanish quiz. Senorita Gonzales gave us a lot of words to learn this week."

"*Sí*," Chloe agreed. "*Muchas palabras.*"

I grinned. Chloe had just said "Yes, many words." And I had understood her. I really liked learning another language. That was one of the cool things about being in middle school — you got to take either French or Spanish as one of your classes. We didn't get to do that back in elementary school.

Chloe pulled out her Spanish binder. It was covered with pictures of Cody Tucker that she'd cut out from magazines and then glued to the binder. I sighed slightly, remembering how Dana Harrison had made fun of Chloe's binder because it wasn't one of the "official" Cody Tucker notebooks. Personally, I thought the colorful, homemade collage on Chloe's binder was nicer than anything I'd seen in a store. But Pops like Dana never appreciated anything that was homemade.

The Pops. That was what my friends and I called Dana and the other popular girls at our school. The Pops aren't actually popular by the dictionary definition, because that would mean they have more friends than anyone else in the school. Actually, they're a very exclusive group. But middle school has its own dictionary. And in our world, the word *popular* has a different definition. It means being a part of the crowd everyone else wishes they could join.

I think every school has its own group of Pops. They're the ones who wear the coolest clothes, have the best makeup, and are so snobby that they only hang out with one another. Basically, they're at the top of the middle school food chain.

No one would call my group of friends Pops. But that's okay with me. Sure I'd love to be considered one of the really cool kids and have everyone want to be like me. But being one of the Pops would mean having to be really vicious to other people all day long the way Dana had been about Chloe's notebook. And that's just not who I am. And I doubt I'll ever change. I've behaved pretty much the same way all my life. I'm just nice Jenny McAfee.

Which is not to say that everyone at our school has always been the way they are now. Middle school definitely changes some people. For example, my BFF all through elementary school was a girl named Addie Wilson. We were inseparable from kindergarten all the way through fifth grade. Then, last summer, while I went away to sleepaway camp, Addie stayed home and became a Pop. By the time we showed up for our first day at Joyce Kilmer Middle School, she had decided we weren't friends anymore. I hadn't had any say in the matter. Basically, what it came down to was she was a Pop and I was not. Pops can't be friends with non-Pops. End of story.

Did I mention that the Pops are a very fickle bunch? In fact, they don't just make fun of other people. They make fun of each other, too, but behind their friends' backs. They make fun of the rest of us to our faces.

My friends and I don't do that. We're really loyal and supportive of one another. That was why I made sure to let Chloe know how much I loved the collage she'd created on her Spanish binder.

"You have a new picture of Cody on there," I said, pointing to the top right-hand corner of the binder, where Chloe had glued a picture of Cody Tucker holding a surfboard.

"Yeah, I found that photo in one of my magazines," Chloe told me. "I'm thinking of learning to surf."

I giggled. "We don't live anywhere near an ocean," I reminded her. "And besides, right now I think we should focus on trying to learn these words." I looked down at my notes. "What does *comida* mean?"

"Food," Chloe said. "Did you know that Cody Tucker's favorite meal is spaghetti and meatballs?"

I shook my head.

"It is. I read it in *Teen Universe Magazine*," Chloe told me. "And in *Teen Scream* it says his favorite color is blue."

"You mean *azul*," I said, using the Spanish word for *blue* in the hopes that Chloe would get the hint and get back to work.

Not a chance. "And in his spare time he likes to surf and ride dirt bikes," Chloe continued.

"Chloe," I said with a heavy sigh. "I don't think there are going to be any questions about Cody Tucker's favorite food on the Spanish quiz."

"Are you trying to tell me that you want to do some more vocabulary?" Chloe asked me.

"That's why I'm here," I replied, trying not to sound too annoyed.

Chloe got the hint. She looked down at her notebook. "What does *ensalada* mean?"

"Salad," I told her.

"Right," she replied.

"How about *bistec*?" I asked her.

"Easy. That's steak," Chloe told me. "Did Senorita Gonzales tell us how to say spaghetti and meatballs?"

I laughed. Chloe had a one-track mind. And it was totally focused on Cody Tucker.

"All this talk about food is making me hungry," Chloe complained. "You wanna go downstairs and raid the refrigerator? I think my mom made a fruit salad with little marshmallows in it."

"Sounds good to me. I love a little *frutas* in the afternoon."

A few minutes later, Chloe and I were sitting in her kitchen, happily munching on apple slices, pineapple bits, and melon chunks.

"I wonder what Cody Tucker is doing right now," Chloe mused as she ate. "Do you think he's eating a fruit salad? Maybe he's writing a new song. That would be great. I love the way he sings."

"And the way he dances, and the way he wears his hair, and the way he smiles," I added, teasing her just a little bit.

"I know," Chloe said. "I'm a little obsessed."

"Just a little," I joked.

"All right, *a lot*," Chloe admitted. "But he's so interesting. And I want to know all I can about him so that when we meet we have something to talk about."

Somehow I doubted Chloe would ever meet Cody Tucker. No one I knew had ever met a star before. But I didn't say that. I didn't want to ruin her dreams. Instead I said, "You're never at a loss for things to say, Chlo."

Chloe laughed. "That's true." Then she paused for a minute. "You have a crush on him, too," she reminded me.

I blushed. Not that that was unusual. It doesn't take much to make me embarrassed. "I guess a little one," I said.

"You like Cody Tucker more than a little," Chloe said.

"I know," I agreed. "But no one likes him as much as you do."

"I know. That's why he and I are made for each other," Chloe said. "I'm the girl for him and I can prove it. Come on." Chloe stood up and headed toward her living room.

"What are we doing?" I asked her.

"We're going on middleschoolsurvival.com," Chloe answered.

I knew that website really well. I'd discovered it during the first week of school. It was filled with quizzes, tips, and advice to help kids get through middle school. I'd used the quizzes on the site to help me make all kinds of decisions, like whether or not I should run for class president (I did, and I won!), and whether I was too addicted to my computer (I was, but I'm cutting back now). But I couldn't figure out what kind of quiz would be able to tell Chloe whether or not she was the perfect girl for Cody Tucker.

"Are you going to take a Cody Tucker trivia test or something?" I asked her.

Chloe shook her head. "Nah. Those don't tell you anything. Anyone who reads the same magazines I do would know those facts. I'm looking for something that says whether or not I'd be a good girlfriend. Cody Tucker is definitely searching for someone he can hang out with and be comfortable with. I read that just yesterday in *Teen Street Magazine.* I need a quiz that will tell me if I'm that kind of girl." She was quiet for a minute as she scrolled down the quiz index on middleschoolsurvival.com. "Okay, here's a good one," she finally said.

What Kind of Girlfriend Are You?

1. **Your school's winter formal is just a few weeks away. Everyone is getting dressed up, but your guy doesn't own a suit. How do you handle the situation?**

   A. Break out all your babysitting money so you can surprise him with a nice sport jacket.
   B. Tell him you don't care what he's wearing. You think he's gorgeous no matter what.
   C. Tell him you want him to go out and get a brand-new suit. You bought a new dress, and you want to be the best-dressed couple at the formal.

Chloe stared at the screen for a minute, thinking. "Well, according to *Teen Dream Magazine*, Cody's not into that whole fancy dress-up thing. And I *do* think he'd look gorgeous in anything. I'm going to click B."

Chloe clicked the mouse once. Then we waited for the next question to pop up on the screen.

2. **Your guy calls sounding very upset. What's your immediate reaction?**

   A. Listen attentively to what's upsetting him and then ask how you can help.

B. Ignore his issues and start right in on how your math teacher totally has it in for you.

C. Fly out the door with your phone in hand and head right for his house.

"C! Totally C!" Chloe exclaimed. "I'm there for Cody whenever he needs me."

I choked back a giggle. I doubted Cody Tucker needed Chloe. He didn't even know she existed. But since this was just a fun quiz, I figured it was okay that she was getting so caught up in it. She clicked the letter C and waited for the next question to appear.

3. It's a girls' day out! You and your besties are hitting the mall hard. While you're there you:

A. Buy yourself a cute pair of jeans, a funky T-shirt, and a new pair of shoes.

B. Buy him a shirt that matches his eyes and two new DVDs you know he's been dying for.

C. Buy yourself a pair of jeans and a new DVD for him.

"This one's harder," Chloe said, staring at the screen. "I mean part of me wants to buy Cody everything, but I also know that he doesn't like girls who are too into material things like gifts. At least that's what it says in all the magazines." She wrinkled her nose for a minute, thinking. Finally she clicked on the letter C. "It's a compromise," she said with a shrug. The next question popped onto the screen.

4. **You and your guy are out to dinner. It's a great time to talk, just the two of you. How does the conversation go?**

   A. You talk for hours, finishing each other's sentences.
   B. You're the one who keeps the conversation going — after all, you have so much more to say than he does.
   C. He does most of the talking, but you don't mind. You can listen to his voice for hours.

"I think I know the answer to this one," Chloe said. "I've imagined it a million times. He and I are on a date. And we're just talking and talking. We each practically know what the other person is thinking. It's definitely A."

She slid the mouse over the letter A, clicked on it, and then moved along with the quiz.

5. **Your guy just lost his after-school job. What's your reaction?**

   A. You wonder how he's going to pay for your Christmas present.
   B. You go with him to the bulletin board in the school hallway to help him look for another job.
   C. You call everyone you know who might need a dog walker or a babysitter so you can help him get a job.

"It's hard to imagine Cody Tucker losing his job," Chloe said. "He's so talented. He'll be popular forever. Still, I guess I have to answer every question. . . ." She scanned the choices carefully. "I would never ask anyone for a present," she told me. "Especially after knowing how hard it is to be out of work."

I nodded understandingly. I knew exactly what Chloe was talking about. Her dad had been out of work for a few weeks earlier this year and money had definitely been tight. Back then she hadn't even wanted to ask her mom for a new dress for a school dance.

"And I can't see Cody as a dog walker," Chloe said. "So I guess the answer is B." She clicked the letter B and waited.

Now it's time to total up your score:

1. A. 1 point
   B. 2 points
   C. 3 points

2. A. 2 points
   B. 3 points
   C. 1 point

3. A. 3 points
    B. 1 point
    C. 2 points

4. A. 2 points
    B. 3 points
    C. 1 point

5. A. 3 points
    B. 2 points
    C. 1 point

You have scored 9 points.
What does your score say about the kind of girlfriend you are?

5–8 points: Uh-oh! You're in danger of becoming a **doormat girlfriend**. While boys might like being the center of your universe for a while, they eventually get tired of it. Worse yet, if you keep going like this, you'll wind up resenting him. It's nice to be considerate of your guy's feelings, but you need to think of yourself, too. He'll respect you more if you do.

9–12 points: You are a **give-and-take girlfriend**, which means you know exactly the kind of balance needed for a healthy relationship in which you both feel comfortable. Congrats!

13-15 points: You are definitely a **pampered princess girlfriend**. Unfortunately, if you think your relationship is all about me, myself, and I, you're likely to wind up alone. Try being as considerate of his needs as you are of your own. You may even find that giving once in a while makes you happier.

Chloe smiled triumphantly. "See, I'm the perfect girlfriend for Cody Tucker," she told me.

"Where does it say that?" I asked her. "I don't see Cody Tucker mentioned anywhere in this whole quiz."

"Well, my score on the quiz does say that I know how to give and take," Chloe told me. "And it says I know how to have a healthy relationship. That means I'm someone Cody can be relaxed around, just like the kind of girlfriend he described in the article. Don't you think Cody deserves a girl like that?"

"I guess so," I replied.

"I *know* so," Chloe told me confidently. "And now that I know I'm the right kind of girl for Cody, all I have to do is meet him." She sighed dreamily. "Maybe we'll meet one day on the red carpet, when we're having our pictures taken."

I smiled. Chloe made it all seem so simple. For a minute I really believed that one day, Chloe would meet Cody Tucker and have her picture taken on the red carpet. And it didn't even seem weird to think that way. That's just the effect Chloe's enthusiasm has on people. When you're around her, you think anything is possible.

Chapter
TWO

CLICK!

The camera's flash surprised me as I walked down the hall with Chloe the next day. No, we weren't on a red carpet. And it wasn't a member of the paparazzi taking our photo. It was my friend Marc. He was taking our picture as we walked toward our lockers in the C wing of Joyce Kilmer Middle School.

"What's this about?" I asked him as I tried to blink away the spots in front of my eyes.

"I'm taking photos for the school yearbook," Marc explained.

"I thought you were in Film Club this year," Chloe said.

"I am," Marc told her. "But I'm helping out with the yearbook. I like taking photos of people, especially candids."

"I don't like candid pictures," Chloe said. "They always catch me off guard."

"That's kind of the point," Marc replied. "It's why they're called candids."

"I've been working on my poses," Chloe said. "You know, in case I ever get famous. Why don't you take one of me opening my locker, like this?"

Chloe opened her locker and started to turn to face the camera when suddenly a pile of textbooks, notebooks, and folders came tumbling out of the locker and onto the floor. Instinctively, Chloe dropped to her knees and began to gather her things.

Click. Marc snapped a picture. "See what I mean?" he asked. "Candid."

Chloe glared up at Marc from the mess on the floor, and I swear I thought I heard her growl at him.

"Don't worry," Marc assured her with a laugh. "I'm deleting it. See?" He held the camera out so Chloe could see the blank screen.

Unfortunately, Chloe couldn't just delete the whole incident — or the fact that Addie Wilson and Dana Harrison were standing nearby when the whole thing happened. They thought it was hilarious — and worth sharing with everyone in the C wing.

"Nice pose," Dana howled.

"Can you do that again so Marc can shoot you from another angle?" Addie asked. She pointed to Chloe's rear end, which was sticking up in the air as she picked up her books. "Maybe get some 'back' lighting?"

As the two Pops waltzed off, I bent down to help Chloe. "Don't worry about them," I told her. "They're just jerks."

"I know," Chloe said. "That doesn't make me mad. What makes me mad is that T-shirt Addie's wearing."

I hadn't noticed the shirt. And I was surprised Chloe had. She never noticed anything anyone wore. Until now.

"It was a brand-new Cody Tucker T-shirt," Chloe continued. "It's one I've never seen before, anywhere. I wonder where she got it."

That explained Chloe's sudden interest in fashion. "Well, you can ask her yourself in a few minutes," I reminded her. "Addie sits right across from you in English class, remember?"

"Oh right, like I'm going to talk to *her*," Chloe said as she picked up the last of her papers. "Even Cody Tucker's not worth that."

"Nice of you two chums to finally get here," my friend Sam greeted Chloe and me in her sophisticated British accent as we hurried into class just a minute before the bell.

"Sorry," I apologized. "Chloe had a slight locker malfunction."

Sam laughed. "I told you to clean out that mess days ago," she said.

"Did we miss anything exciting?" I asked Sam.

She shook her head. "No. Just Dana talking about some horror movie she went to see last night with her brother. From what she was saying, it sounds like it was just one grotty murder after another."

"I bet it's that movie where the guy who's dressed as

Santa Claus goes around murdering a bunch of teenagers," I said. "My parents won't let me see it."

"My mum and dad nixed it, too," Sam told me.

"Almost everyone's parents did," Chloe said. "Which is probably why Dana was talking about it in front of everyone. She was just bragging — for a change. That's all those Pops do — brag, brag, brag."

Just then Ms. Jaffe, our English teacher, walked into the room. She stood at the blackboard and smiled at us. "Good morning, everyone. Please take out your homework."

I pulled out my homework folder and took out a single piece of paper. The homework last night hadn't been hard. All we had to do was read one chapter and answer a few short questions. No big deal.

Ms. Jaffe walked around the room, scanning the papers on our desks. She stopped when she reached Dana's desk. There was no paper out. Instead, Dana was busy rummaging through her binder.

"I don't know where my homework went," she told Ms. Jaffe. "But I did it. Maybe it's in my locker. Or it could be in a different binder. I'll give it to you tomorrow."

Sam, Chloe, and I shared knowing glances. We all knew Dana was lying. She had been at the movies last night. She was just putting on a big show of looking for her homework so Ms. Jaffe would give her an extra night to get it done. Dana had obviously not learned one of the big unwritten rules of middle school.

MIDDLE SCHOOL RULE #36:

DON'T LIE ABOUT HAVING DONE YOUR HOMEWORK WHEN YOU HAVEN'T. TEACHERS ARE NEVER FOOLED.

Ms. Jaffe studied Dana's face for a minute, and then began collecting everyone else's homework papers. "Don't worry about it, Dana, I believe you," she said.

I was shocked. I was sure that Middle School Rule #36 always held true. Was it possible one of the Pops could break an unwritten rule and get away with it? *Why not?* They always seemed to get special treatment.

But then Ms. Jaffe continued talking. "And since you did your homework, you won't have any trouble with the pop quiz I've just decided to give."

"Grrr. Thanks a lot, Dana," Justin Abrams groaned from the back row. And he wasn't the only one who seemed angry with Dana. The whole class was grumbling.

But Ms. Jaffe ignored our complaints. "For those of you who read the chapter and did the homework, this should be easy. I will ask you two of the five questions you answered last night. Just write down your answers on a piece of blank paper," she said.

Suddenly I felt better. That was pretty easy — especially as pop quizzes go. I relaxed a little in my chair. But out of the corner of my eye, I could see Dana wasn't relaxed at all. Her jaw was clenched and her face had gone white. She was about to be caught in her lie and she knew it. Now she would have a zero for her homework and probably a failing quiz grade, too.

I know it's not nice to be happy when someone else gets in trouble, but I couldn't help it — especially after the way Dana had been treating Chloe. I have to admit I was kind of happy to see a Pop popped by a pop quiz!

The English quiz wasn't the last one I had that morning. My math teacher had also surprised us with one on changing fractions to decimals. By the time I got to lunch I was ready for the break.

"Rough morning?" my friend Liza asked as she sat down next to me at lunch.

"How could you tell?" I asked her.

"You look tired," she said. "Usually you're more perky."

I laughed. *Perky* was a word people had used to describe me for years. I like to smile at people, and I try to be friendly. But right now, I was totally wiped out.

I looked across the table toward my friend Josh. He was busy working out some math problems while he ate his lunch. I was surprised because Josh wasn't the type to forget to do his homework.

"Do you have a math test today, too?" I asked Josh. He wasn't in my math class. Even though Josh is in sixth grade, he's taking seventh grade math. He's sort of a genius, at least when it comes to math.

"No," Josh answered. "I'm studying for the Mathletes competition tomorrow. We're up against Roosevelt Middle School, and they're pretty tough."

"Our team will win," Liza assured him. "You're their secret weapon."

Josh blushed slightly and shook his head. "I don't know. We're both undefeated teams. Do you guys want to come and cheer us on?"

We all looked strangely at Josh. Apparently none of us could figure out how you would cheer at a Mathletes competition. Besides, I couldn't go even if I wanted to.

"I have a student council meeting tomorrow," I told him. "We're planning the Winter Formal."

"Oh, that," Marc said with a dismissive tone.

"What's wrong with the Winter Formal?" Chloe asked him.

"Nothing," Marc said. "It's just not anything special." Like Liza, Marc is a seventh grader, so while things like the Winter Formal are new to me, they're old news to him.

Just then my friends Marilyn and Carolyn came over to the table. They both put their trays down at the exact same time, smiled at us, and asked in unison, "What are we talking about?"

"I love the twin thing," Chloe told them with a grin.

"We're talking about the Winter Formal," Sam told the twins. "Marc's not exactly gobsmacked over it."

"Last year's was really boring," Carolyn told her.

"Just another school dance with nicer clothing," Marilyn added.

"This year's will be better," I told my seventh grade friends in a voice that I hoped was filled with confidence. "We're brainstorming ideas to make it special. I'll let you know what we come up with."

"And let me know when they've scheduled you for your group photograph," Marc said. "I think I was assigned the student council."

"What group photograph?" I asked him.

"For the yearbook," Marc explained. "Every club, group, or team at school gets their picture taken for the activities section."

Liza giggled. "You remember that eighth grader, Jessie, from last year?" she asked Marc and the twins.

"Oh right!" Carolyn replied. "She was in, like, four activities."

"I think she broke the record for most pictures in one yearbook," Marilyn added.

"Years from now, people will probably think she was some kind of celebrity," Marc said with a laugh.

I could see Chloe perk up at the sound of the word *celebrity.* But before she could ask any questions or make a comment, a parade of Pops passed by our table. They pass us every day on the way to the girls' room, which is where the Pops gather during lunch. It's sort of like their clubhouse. They go to the bathroom and put on their makeup and gossip about people until lunch is over.

Usually, the Pops stop by our table and make some nasty comment about what one of us is wearing, or eating, or saying. But today, they just walked by. As they passed I could hear Addie saying, "And when my dad brought home this Cody Tucker T-shirt I was so surprised. No one else has one yet. They don't actually go on sale for another week."

Obviously the Pops were more interested in Addie's Cody Tucker shirt than in making fun of us.

"Are you going into their 'clubhouse' to take a picture of their 'club,' too, Marc?" Sam teased him as the Pops paraded by.

"No thanks," he answered. "I'm staying as far from them as possible."

We all nodded in agreement. Staying away from the Pops was an activity we all participated in. We just didn't get our pictures in the yearbook for it.

Unfortunately, there was no way I could stay away from Addie and Dana for very long. They were in my gym class, and that meant I had to spend an entire period playing badminton with them. Well, *I* was playing badminton. They were just standing there with their rackets, talking. I could hear their entire conversation. I wasn't actually eavesdropping, though, because they were talking really loudly. Knowing Addie, she wanted everyone in our gym class to know what she was saying. Not that I blamed her. What she was talking about was actually really cool.

"My dad's company is sponsoring Cody Tucker's tour," she told Dana.

"You're kidding!" Dana exclaimed, impressed.

"That's why I've got the new T-shirt," Addie explained. "It's only supposed to be sold in the arenas where Cody plays. But my dad brought one home from the office for me."

"Does your dad actually know Cody Tucker?" Dana asked.

Addie didn't answer right away. Then she said, "Sure. Everyone at his company does. That's why I'm going to get amazing seats when Cody performs here."

"When's Cody performing here?" Dana wondered.

"I don't know," Addie admitted.

Dana didn't say anything. And she looked a little less impressed until Addie spoke again. "Cody's coming to town next week for a meeting at my dad's company," Addie said. "But don't tell anyone. It's supposed to be a secret."

I had to laugh a little at that one. Some secret. Addie had practically broadcast it across the entire gym. How typical.

Chapter
THREE

"OUR STUDENT COUNCIL yearbook photo session is next Friday," Sandee Wind, the eighth grade class president, announced during our meeting the following afternoon. "Now, does anybody have any new business before we start planning the Winter Formal?"

I looked around the table. Everyone looked a little bored. Everyone but Addie and me, that is. As the sixth grade representatives, we were excited about planning our first formal dance. But like Marc, Liza, and the twins, none of the seventh or eighth graders seemed all that thrilled about it.

"What's there to plan?" John Benson, the eighth grade vice president, asked Sandee. "It's going to be exactly the same as last year's Winter Formal. And the one the year before that."

Now I was getting kind of bummed out. Ever since I'd heard about the Winter Formal, I'd been imagining a magical night, with everyone all dressed up, dancing under shimmering wintry decorations, and drinking hot cider, while some really cool band plays hit songs. You know, like you see in the movies or on TV.

But apparently that wasn't what the Winter Formal was like at our school.

"I guess we could hire Mr. Wilke to do the DJ stuff again," Kia Samson, the seventh grade class president, said with a sigh.

"But he plays classic rock," Sandee reminded her. "I don't think anyone wants to dance to eighties music. Yuck. My *parents* danced to that stuff."

"Well, who else can we get to do it?" Kia asked Sandee.

"Do we have to have a DJ?" I asked. "Wouldn't a band be more fun?"

Sandee nodded. "It would." She turned to Addie. "That band you got us from the high school for the first dance of the year was great," she said.

Addie sat up proudly and smiled. "Thanks," she said. "They played as a personal favor to me."

I rolled my eyes. That was such an Addie thing to say. Not that I could argue with her. It was exactly what had happened. Addie had definitely saved that dance by bringing in live music.

"Do you think they'd do it again?" Sandee asked her.

"No," Addie said, slumping back down in her chair like a deflated balloon. "Their bass player flunked geometry and he's grounded. No more gigs until he gets his grades up."

"That's the problem with a high school band," I said. "It's too bad we can't get someone professional. Someone who is really talented, but doesn't have to ask permission to play a gig."

Sandee nodded. "That would be great," she agreed. "But who knows anyone like that?"

"Seriously, Jenny," Addie said with a sarcastic laugh. "Where would a bunch of middle school kids meet a talented, professional musician?"

I frowned. Addie never passed up a chance to make it seem as though my ideas were idiotic, especially at student council meetings. She was still angry that I'd been voted sixth grade class president and she was only vice president. So she made it her business to show me up whenever she could. If only I knew someone who knew someone who was a professional musician . . .

Suddenly it came to me. A solution so simple, I was surprised Addie hadn't volunteered it herself. Especially since *she* was the person who knew someone who knew a musician!

"Why don't you ask your dad to ask Cody Tucker if he would play at our dance?" I suggested to Addie.

Everyone in the room leaped to attention. No one looked bored anymore. Everyone seemed thrilled and amazed. Everyone but Addie, that is.

"What are you talking about, Jenny?" she asked me nervously.

"Your dad works for the company that sponsors Cody's tour, right?" I asked her excitedly.

"Well, yeah, but . . ." Addie started.

"And you said your dad knew him, right?" I continued. "I heard you telling Dana about it in gym class."

"Why were you eavesdropping on our conversation?" Addie demanded.

"I wasn't," I said. "I was just standing right near you when you were talking."

"Well, then you heard me tell Dana it was a secret," Addie told me.

Suddenly I felt really uncomfortable. I hadn't meant to tell Addie's secret. But she'd been talking so loudly, I figured the other people in our gym class knew it, too. "I figured you'd bring it up, anyway, as soon as you thought of it," I told her. "You're the one who always does everything to make the dances great." I added that last part to make her feel good — and to make her stop shooting imaginary daggers at me with her eyes.

"Is it true, Addie?" Kia asked her. "Does your dad really know Cody Tucker?"

"Um . . . yeah," Addie said nervously. "But I don't think . . ."

"Addie, if you could get Cody Tucker to sing even one song at our school dance, you would be a legend!" Sandee exclaimed. "Our school would be written up in the papers."

"We might even get some TV shows to come and film our dance," I said.

"It would definitely make this Winter Formal different from all the others," Ethan added.

"Well, I guess I could ask my dad to find out if Cody Tucker could sing just one song," Addie said. "But I can't promise anything. I mean, Cody's a busy guy."

"We know," Sandee told her. "And if he can't do it, we'll understand."

"I'm just excited to know someone who knows Cody Tucker," Kia said with a sigh. "Addie, you're so lucky."

Addie smiled at her. "I know. Did you see the shirt I was wearing yesterday? That's from Cody's tour. They're not even on sale yet, but my dad was able to get it for me."

From that moment on, there was no new business at our student council meeting. All anyone was talking about was Cody Tucker – even the boys. And Addie was just where she loved to be, at the center of it all.

That's why I couldn't understand why Addie was so mean to me in the parking lot while she and I waited for the late bus.

"I can't believe you did that, Jenny McAfee," she snarled.

"What?" I asked her. "You want the Winter Formal to be good, don't you? Besides, you would have thought of it in a minute. After all, Cody Tucker is *your* dad's friend."

"I wouldn't say they're friends. . . ." Addie began.

"But he knows him, right?"

Addie shrugged. "It's none of your business," she told me. "And it wasn't up to you to bring Cody Tucker and my dad up in the meeting. It was my place to do that."

So that was what this was all about. Addie thought I was going to get the credit for having Cody Tucker at our dance. But I didn't care about stuff like that. I just wanted to have a great dance.

"No one even remembers I'm the one who said anything," I assured Addie. "Everyone is giving you the credit."

"*If* I can get him," Addie reminded me.

Before I could answer that, I saw Chloe walking into the parking lot to wait for the late bus. That was odd. Now that the school musical was over, Chloe didn't have any after-school activities.

"Excuse me, Addie," I said quickly. "I've gotta go talk to Chloe." I smiled as I hurried over to Chloe. I was happy for the excuse to get away from an argument with Addie.

"What are you doing here?" I asked Chloe as I caught up to her.

"The team had practice," Chloe said.

I looked at her strangely. As far as I knew, Chloe didn't play any sports. "What team?" I asked her.

"The wrestling team," she told me.

"Wrestling?" I repeated. Now I was *totally* confused. At our school, wrestling is a boys' sport.

"I'm their equipment manager," Chloe explained.

"Since when?" I asked. Chloe had never mentioned it to me before.

"I just started today," she told me. "We have our first meet next Monday."

"Oh," I said, still confused. *What was this all about?*

"And then we have our yearbook photos taken one week from tomorrow," she continued. "That's a good thing because I'm having my office assistants yearbook photo and our buddy mentoring group photo taken the same day, so I only have to pick out one outfit for three photos. But I still have photo sessions on—"

"When did you become an office assistant?" I asked, interrupting her.

"I volunteered today," she explained. "I'm going to work there twice a week."

"When?"

"During my study hall periods on Tuesdays and Thursdays," she said. "And Thursday is the day they take the picture."

"How many yearbook pictures are you going to be in, Chloe?" I asked.

"Well, there's the cast shot of *You're a Good Man, Charlie Brown*," she replied, talking about the school musical she'd been in earlier in the year. "And then the wrestling team photo, and the office assistants photo, the buddy mentoring volunteers photo, and of course our individual photos. So that's five . . . so far."

"So far?" I asked her.

Chloe nodded. "I still need one more to beat the record for most photos in the yearbook. I love having my picture taken. It makes me feel like a celebrity. They have their pictures taken all the time."

So that was it. Chloe was joining all these groups just so she could beat Jessie-the-eighth-grader's record for most yearbook pictures. But I had a feeling Chloe was going to be sorry about joining all these activities at once. After all, she was breaking a major unwritten middle school rule.

MIDDLE SCHOOL RULE #37:

DON'T OVERLOAD YOUR SCHEDULE WITH TOO MANY ACTIVITIES. YOUR SCHOOLWORK IS SURE TO SUFFER.

"Chloe, you're going to have a lot of homework if you give up your study hall periods," I said. "Study hall is when everyone gets a start on their homework."

"It's not a big deal," Chloe said. "I can handle it."

"But, Chlo . . ." I began. Unfortunately, my voice was drowned out by the sound of the late buses pulling into the parking lot.

"Oh, there's my bus," Chloe shouted. "Gotta run. See you tomorrow, Jen."

Chapter
FOUR

I WAS ALMOST LATE to the bus the next day. I overslept and then I couldn't find my gloves or my warm, wool hat. I'd had to throw on any old hat and gloves, and then I had to race like crazy to catch the bus.

My stomach didn't feel so great as I ran. Not only had I eaten my cereal way too fast, I was also pretty nervous about what would happen when I reached the bus stop. I was certain Addie would already be there, and she was sure to have a great time making fun of my purple-and-yellow ski cap and brown gloves, which not only didn't match each other but didn't match my blue jacket, either. I thought about taking off the hat and gloves and throwing them in my backpack before I reached the bus stop, but it was too cold to be outside without them. So I was going to have to accept the fact that I'd be giving Addie a good laugh that day.

But Addie didn't laugh. At least not out loud, anyway. In fact, when she saw me, she turned her back without saying a word. I figured she must've been on the phone telling one of the Pops – probably Maya or Claire – all about the horrible mess Jenny McAfee was this morning. But when the bus pulled up and Addie turned around, I could see she wasn't even holding her phone. She was simply ignoring me. That was weird. It was nice for a change. But it was weird just the same.

I climbed into my usual seat and looked out the window as the bus pulled away from the stop. A few minutes later we stopped at the corner near my friend Felicia's house. As Felicia got on the bus, I moved over to let her sit down.

"Cool button," I said when I noticed the huge CODY TUCKER 4EVER button she'd attached to her backpack.

"Thanks," Felicia said. "I found it at the mall. I'm going to see if he'll sign it for me."

"When would he do that?" I asked her.

"At the dance," Felicia answered. She sounded kind of surprised I'd even asked. Then she turned around and smiled at Addie. "I can't believe you're going to get Cody Tucker to come to the Winter Formal," she said. "That's the greatest thing anyone has ever done!"

Addie turned ghostly white, but her expression didn't change at all. She just kept scowling at Felicia and me the way she usually did when we dared to speak to her royal Popness.

"Where did you hear that?" Addie demanded. She glared in my direction.

"Don't look at *me*," I said. "I haven't said a word to anyone."

"Kia told Cathy Donovan," Felicia explained. "And Cathy told Rachel. Rachel called me right away when she heard." She turned to me. "I would have called you, but I figured you already knew, since Addie brought it up at the student council meeting."

I figured Addie would be pretty happy to hear that. After all, like I'd predicted, she'd gotten credit for the idea. But surprisingly, Addie didn't look happy at all.

Addie didn't say another word the entire bus ride. She just sat there, staring out the window, making it a point to ignore everyone else on the bus. That wasn't unusual, though. Addie is the only Pop on our bus. She never sits with any of us non-Pops, and she rarely speaks to us, either.

But that didn't stop everyone else on the bus from talking. We were all buzzing about the Winter Formal.

"What are you going to wear?" Felicia asked me. "I was thinking of wearing the purple velvet dress I wore to my aunt's wedding a few weeks ago, but now I don't know if it's special enough."

"Not special enough?" I repeated, surprised. "That was a really fancy wedding."

"I know, but this is Cody Tucker!" Felicia exclaimed.

I knew what she meant. It isn't every day a celebrity comes to a middle school dance. Everyone was really psyched. I had to hand it to Addie. She was really coming through for us this time. Pop or no Pop, I was really glad she went to my school — at least for now.

And I wasn't the only one who felt that way. As soon as our bus pulled into the school parking lot, a crowd of kids gathered near the door. They waited patiently as Felicia and I and a couple of other kids got off. But when Addie stepped down onto the cement, they crowded around her, cheering wildly. Apparently everyone in the whole school knew about what had happened at the student council meeting.

"Addie, you rock!" A tall boy who I thought must be an eighth grader complimented her.

"Can I touch you?" a short, redheaded girl asked.

"Why would you want to do that?" Addie wondered.

"Because then I'll have touched someone who knows Cody Tucker," the girl explained.

Addie smiled and benevolently put out her hand. "Go ahead, then," she said, sounding like a queen speaking to one of her subjects.

Suddenly I heard some weird clicking sounds. Cameras! People were taking pictures of Addie. Addie had heard the clicking noises, too. I could tell by the fake picture-taking smile she plastered on her face as she looked around at her adoring public.

There was one person who was not cheering for Addie. I could see Chloe staring at her from the outskirts of the crowd. She did not look impressed.

"What's up, Chlo?" I asked as I walked over to join her.

"Do you believe this?" Chloe asked me. "They're taking a million pictures of her. It's like she's the celebrity or something, instead of Cody."

I had a feeling Chloe was upset by something more than just the injustice to Cody Tucker. My guess was that Chloe was jealous that Addie was getting all the attention she always wanted for herself.

"Well, at least we'll get to see Cody Tucker close up," I said, trying to help her cheer up. "Your dream will finally come true."

"We'll see," Chloe said.

"What do you mean?" I asked her.

"Oh, come on, Jenny," Chloe said. "You don't believe that Addie Wilson is going to be able to get Cody Tucker to come to the dance, do you? She probably doesn't even know him."

"Her *dad* knows him," I told Chloe. "I heard her telling Dana all about it. Why would she lie to one of her best friends about something like that?"

"Why does Addie Wilson do anything?" Chloe asked me. "To show off. To sound important."

I thought about that for a minute. Chloe was right. Addie did show off a lot. Could it be that she was showing off this time, too? I looked over toward the crowd of kids who were surrounding her. If she was showing off, there were going to be a whole lot of disappointed Cody Tucker fans at our middle school.

And that included my friends. At just that moment, Rachel and the twins came over to talk to Chloe and me. They seemed pretty excited about the whole Cody Tucker thing.

"Do you guys know why musicians like Cody Tucker are so sweet?" Rachel asked us.

I had a feeling this was one of Rachel's jokes and not a serious question. So I just said, "No, why?"

"Because they have *jam* sessions," Rachel answered. Then she started laughing at her own joke.

I forced myself to give a little laugh, too, although the joke wasn't all that funny. I just didn't want Rachel to feel bad.

"I hate to admit it, but Addie Wilson did something good this time," Carolyn said, focusing the attention off of Rachel's bad joke and back onto Addie and her fans.

"Mega-good," Marilyn agreed. "Great, even."

"Did Addie say whether or not we were going to get to meet Cody Tucker?" Carolyn asked me.

"Or is he just going to sing and leave?" Marilyn wondered.

"Addie didn't exactly say Cody was definitely coming," I explained to the twins. "She just said she would try to —"

But my friends didn't hear what I was saying. My words were drowned out by the crowd cheering around Addie. Which was just as well, I guess. Marilyn and Carolyn wouldn't have wanted to hear that Addie hadn't guaranteed anything yet. Like everyone else in school, they just wanted to hear that Cody Tucker would be at our Winter Formal.

*　　*　　*

Surprisingly, Chloe was the only person who didn't seem to have Cody Tucker on her mind at lunch. Instead, she was focused on the paper plates and plastic bottles on our lunch trays.

"Do you know how long it will take for those plastic bottles to decompose in a landfill?" she demanded.

"About a thousand years," Josh replied matter-of-factly.

"Is there anything you *don't* know?" Sam asked him jokingly.

"I don't know why Chloe is asking us about this," Josh replied with a laugh.

"I'm asking because I'm on a mission to save the planet," Chloe told him. "All of us in the Environment Club are."

"Since when are you in the Environment Club?" Marc asked her.

"Since I signed up online last night," Chloe replied. "I just e-mailed Alison Corbin and asked her if she needed any help. She e-mailed me back this whole page of information about what we can do to save the planet."

"Another club?" I asked Chloe. "How many are you going to join?"

"I didn't even know you could join clubs now. I thought you had to do that during sign-up week at the beginning of the school year," Sam said.

Liza shook her head. "Some clubs let you join later, if they need more members or if they need help with a special project."

"Exactly," Chloe agreed. "The wrestling team needed an equipment manager, and they always need help in the office. And the Environment Club is looking for new members."

"I didn't know you were so into ecology and sports," Sam said. "I thought you were more into theater stuff."

"Can I help it if I have a lot of interests?" Chloe replied.

I knew Chloe's *real* interest was getting photographed for the yearbook. But I didn't say that. Why embarrass her in front of all of our friends? Besides, Chloe wasn't letting any of us get a word in, anyway.

"This school is just destroying the environment in so many ways," she continued. "Like, take how hot it is in here, for instance. We don't need all this heat. We can wear sweaters or sweatshirts and lower the temperature a little bit. I'm in a T-shirt and I'm sweating."

My mind drifted off a bit as Chloe continued on her ecology lecture. Instead of thinking about plastic bottles, recycled paper, and the school temperature, my mind had returned to the conversation Felicia and I had had on the bus earlier that day. I needed a new dress for the Winter Formal. Well, I didn't exactly need one—I wanted one. I only hoped I could convince my mom and dad that this dance was important enough for a new dress.

My mom was surprisingly easy to convince. In fact, when I brought up the idea of buying a dress, she pulled out some old photo albums and began reminiscing about *her* first Winter Formal.

"This is what I wore to my middle school Winter Formal," my mom told me as she pointed to an old picture of herself. "Of course, I was in seventh grade then. And they called it junior high, not middle school. But it was the same thing."

Seeing pictures of my parents when they were young is always bizarre. When I look at the photos, I can sort of see the same faces they have now—the eyes haven't changed, and their smiles are the ones I'm familiar with. But the hair and the clothes—yikes! Back in middle school, my mom had really big hair! I mean *huge.* Her hair is naturally straight, like mine. But in these pictures, it was really, really curly.

"I can't believe I got that perm," my mom laughed. "I thought I looked gorgeous. Hard to imagine looking at it now, huh?"

I laughed. The perm was pretty bad. Her dress wasn't so great, either. It was this shimmery purple knee-length dress with big puffy sleeves and a huge bow across the chest. My mom must have noticed the expression on my face because she laughed a little and said, "Believe it or not, this was the style back then. But don't worry, we'll get you something a little more modern at the mall tomorrow."

"Thanks," I told her.

"Do you have any idea what you're looking for?" my mom asked.

I shook my head. "I've never had a formal dress before," I told her. "I'm not sure what would look best."

"We'll figure it out tomorrow," my mom assured me. "If I could find a dress for my first Winter Formal, we can find one for you, too."

I wasn't about to leave choosing my first Winter Formal dress in the hands of a woman who had once had a puffy perm that went with the puffy sleeves on her dress. So before I went to bed, I logged onto middleschoolsurvival.com for advice on the kind of dress that would look best on me. And sure enough, there was a whole article about how to pick out the right dress for a formal dance.

Formal Fashion Dos and Don'ts

Congratulations! You're about to go to your first middle school formal. How exciting! How *stressful*!

Obviously, the most stressful part is finding the perfect outfit. But if you just follow these simple tips, shopping for your dream dress will be easy.

1. Before you head to the mall, look through magazines to see what kinds of dresses you like. That way, when you get to the store, you have a starting point.

2. Think about your body type. If you have really nice shoulders or a long neck, try a dress with spaghetti straps to accentuate your best features. If you have long, lean legs, but are a little thick around the tummy, try a dress with a skirt that starts just below the thickest part of your waist to make your middle look slimmer. If your stomach is your best feature, try a classic A-line look that clings to your middle and then fans out into a full skirt.

3. Decide what kind of image you're trying to convey with your dress. If you want to look ready for fun, go for bright colors, like a fiery red or a sunshine yellow. Going for a mysterious look? Then try on dresses that are darker in color, such as mauve, brown,

purple, or black. If you want to look very grownup, ivory or white will do the trick.

4. Don't buy the first dress you fall in love with — at least not until you've tried on three or four others. Trying on dresses in other colors and styles will either convince you that the first dress is perfect, or show you that you need to try something else.

I sat back for a minute and thought about what I had just read, especially that last part about what the differently colored dresses meant. Exactly what kind of image *did* I want to project at the Winter Formal?

Right away I knew I could forget about wearing a white or ivory dress. I can be a total klutz. Put me in white and I'd be likely to spill punch all over myself.

However, if I did get to meet Cody Tucker, it would be cool for him to think I was mysterious and sophisticated. After all, those are probably the kinds of people he meets at the Hollywood parties he goes to. But I'm not a singing star or a movie star. I'm in middle school. And I had a feeling that no dress was going to make me seem more sophisticated than any other sixth grader. Besides, the truth was, I wanted to have fun at my first formal. So I was going to look for dresses that were bright red or yellow. After all, why shouldn't I look like someone who was ready to have a good time? That's who I was!

FIVE

"THIS BROWN DRESS is really sweet," my mom said as we worked our way through the racks of dresses at one of the little boutiques in our mall the next morning.

I shook my head. "I told you, I don't want a dark color. I want a really bright dress," I said. Then I stopped myself. I knew I sounded tired and cranky, probably because I *was* tired and cranky. But so was my mom. And she was doing this for me. So I added, "I mean, I really want something a little less intense."

My mother nodded. "Gotcha," she said. "More playful."

I looked at her with surprise. Had mom been reading middleschoolsurvival.com? No. That wasn't possible. My mom hardly ever searched the Internet.

"How about this one?" she asked, holding up a bright red sleeveless dress with a really full skirt and a bright blue sash around the middle.

"That's the one!" I gingerly fingered the thick, shimmery material. "I have to have it!"

My mother laughed. "Don't you think you should try it on first?" she asked me.

"Oh, yeah, right," I replied sheepishly. "That would be

a good idea." I took the dress from her and hurried over to the dressing room.

As I slipped out of my jeans and T-shirt for, like, the eleventh time, my stomach rumbled. I was definitely getting hungry. Trying on clothes is sort of like working out. After a while you need a rush of carbs if you're going to keep at it.

But all thoughts of food rushed out of my brain as I looked at my reflection in the mirror. The red dress fit me perfectly. It wasn't too tight or too big. The skirt was a little longer than I was used to — it went below my knees — but somehow that made it feel more formal. And when I twirled around, it ballooned up like a shimmery red tulip, just like I'd imagined.

"I love it!" I shouted as I literally danced out of the dressing room to show my mother.

I was kind of surprised at my mother's reaction. I thought she'd be really excited about how I looked in it — or at least happy that I'd finally found something I liked. But she just stood there, staring at me with this odd, blank look on her face.

"Are you okay?" I asked her.

She nodded and then gave me a funny little smile. "You just look really grownup, that's all. It's kind of a shock. Your first formal dress . . . "

I blushed, realizing how many of the women around us had heard her. I could see them all smiling at me with the same expression people use when they see a little girl playing dress up. But I *wasn't* a little girl, and this wasn't dress up. This was the real thing. How embarrassing!

"Um . . . well . . . um, do you think we should get this one?" I asked my mom. "Because I'm kind of hungry."

My mother nodded. "We should definitely get this dress. And then we should get some lunch."

I breathed a sigh of relief as I hurried back into the dressing room. I was glad to get away from all the adults who were smiling at me. I was also really happy to have found the perfect dress. Now, more than ever, I was totally psyched for our Winter Formal. This day was turning out to be a real success!

Unfortunately, things took a definite turn for the worse when my mom and I got to the food court. I was just sitting there, munching on my cheeseburger, when suddenly I spotted three Pops — Maya, Dana, and Claire — walking toward a nearby table. They all had trays of food with them, so I knew they were in the food court to stay. This time they weren't just passing by on the way to the bathroom, like they would've been if we had been in the school cafeteria.

I sat there, trying to hide behind the bun of my burger, praying they wouldn't see me. And for a while, I thought I'd gotten away with it. They were so busy talking to each other about whatever it is that Pops talk about, that they didn't seem to notice anyone else in the food court.

"I'm going to go get a cup of coffee," my mom said. "Do you want anything? Maybe a cinnamon bun or a pretzel for dessert?"

I shook my head. "I'm fine," I told her. "In fact, I'm kind of tired. Do you want to go home? You could have coffee there."

"Did you forget that we still have to get you shoes?" my mother asked me. "Your good shoes don't fit you anymore. And that dress won't look very good with sneakers."

Darn. I'd totally forgotten about the shoes. There was no way I was going home now.

As my mom got up from the table, I turned my body slightly so that the Pops couldn't see my face. From the back I could be just about any sixth grader with straight brown hair.

Unfortunately, the Pops had already spotted me from the front. And a minute later Dana was standing at my table. "Jenny McAfee, what are *you* doing here?" she asked me in a tone that made it sound like I had absolutely no right to be in the same mall as her.

"I was shopping, and now I'm eating lunch. What else would I be doing at a mall?" I knew I sounded a little mean, but I didn't care. Dana had sounded mean first.

Dana looked around. "Who are you here with?" she asked me.

"My mom," I told her.

"Oh," Dana said. She let out a little laugh.

"What's so funny?" I asked her.

"Nothing," Dana said. "It's just that you still come to the mall with your mom."

"Don't you?" I asked her.

Dana shook her head. "Claire, Maya, and I are here *by ourselves*. We don't need our moms to hold our hands in the mall. But I guess you do."

"I don't hold my mother's hand," I answered.

The minute the words were out of my mouth I regretted them. I knew that wasn't what Dana had meant. She'd meant that going to the mall alone was something you do when you're in middle school.

"Oh, Jenny, you're so pathetic," Dana said. "But don't worry. I won't tell any of your friends you were here with your *mother,* I promise."

As Dana turned and walked away, I knew I was in for big trouble when I got back to school on Monday. Of course, Dana wouldn't tell any of my friends she'd seen me here with my mom. She never spoke to my friends. But I knew she'd spread the word to the Pops. In fact, judging by the way she, Maya, and Claire were giggling into their cell phones, the word was already spreading.

That night, I called Rachel. She, Felicia, and I had all gone to elementary school together, so it just seemed natural for me to call her when I was freaking out about something. (Addie and Dana had gone to school with us, too, but I never called them about anything.) I just had to know if I was the only kid in the school who had to go to the mall with an adult.

"Hey, Jen, what's up?" Rachel asked as she answered the phone.

"I got my dress today," I told her. "It's amazing."

"Wow, you're so lucky!" Rachel exclaimed. "My mom can't take me shopping until the middle of next week. By then all the good dresses will be gone."

I laughed. "Don't worry, there are a million dresses at the mall," I told her. "I think I tried them all on today."

"You must be beat," Rachel said. "My mom makes me try on a lot of stuff before we buy anything, too."

"So you always go to the mall with your mom?" I asked her.

"Sure," Rachel said. "I'm not going to go with my dad. He has terrible taste."

"No, I mean, do you ever go to the mall without a parent?" I asked her. "Just you and a friend?"

"I'm not allowed to," Rachel told me. "Are you?"

"No," I said. "You know my mom, she's a worrier."

"Mine, too," Rachel said. "I think all moms are."

"Not Dana's mom," I said. Then I told her about what had happened to me in the food court.

"Wow, that must've been embarrassing," Rachel said sympathetically when I'd finished my story.

"You have no idea," I told her. "And it's going to get worse on Monday, when she tells everyone."

"Who's going to care?" Rachel asked me. "Hardly anyone I know gets to go to the mall alone. And so what if they do? Does that make them some sort of advanced geniuses? Come on, Jenny. Nothing is going to make Dana superior to *you*."

I smiled. Good old Rachel. She always knew what to say to cheer me up.

"Speaking of parents, are you going to work with your dad on Wednesday?" Rachel continued.

"Why would I do that?" I asked her.

"It's Bring Your Child to the Office day," Rachel explained. "I'm going with my mom. Her office is having all sorts of programs to show us what our parents do for a living."

"My dad's office does that, too," I told her. "I went last year. But I think my dad is out of town a couple of days this week. He travels a lot for work."

"Yeah, I know," Rachel said. "Too bad you have to go to school on Wednesday, though."

"Nah. It's okay," I told her. "Last year I had to write a paper about what my experience at my dad's office was like. I don't want to have to write an extra paper. Besides, his office is boring."

"It can't be any more boring than school," Rachel pointed out.

"That's true," I agreed.

"So tell me about the new dress," Rachel said.

We spent the next few minutes talking about my new red party dress, and whether or not Rachel should go for a dark, mysterious dress or a white, sophisticated one. By the time we hung up, I was feeling really happy again. After all, what did I have to be upset about? So Dana had seen me at the mall with my mom. My friends wouldn't tease me or look down on me because of it. They weren't like that. I had the best friends in the world. And we were going to hear Cody Tucker singing at the Winter Formal together. I decided that I wasn't going to let anything bring me down.

That all changed on Sunday afternoon when I overheard my mom having a phone conversation with Mrs. Wilson. I heard her say, "What made Addie promise to do something like that?"

My ears definitely perked up at the sound of Addie's name. I knew I shouldn't have been eavesdropping, but I couldn't stop myself.

"I know the kids would have loved to have him sing at their dance," my mother continued. "But Addie couldn't have seriously believed Pete would be able to get that for her. Cody Tucker is a huge star. Why would Addie think they even knew each other?"

Suddenly I got a sick feeling in the pit of my stomach. Pete was Addie's father's name. And from the sound of the conversation, he wasn't nearly as close to Cody Tucker as Addie had made it seem.

This was awful! We weren't going to have Cody Tucker at our school dance. Everyone was going to be really disappointed.

Somehow, I had a feeling Addie wasn't going to take the blame. She was going to have to make this someone else's fault. And considering how much she hated me, I had a sneaking suspicion the "someone" she was going to push the blame onto was me.

Chapter
SIX

I WAS RIGHT. On Monday morning, Addie was waiting for me at the bus stop. From the look on her face, I could tell she was furious.

"Jenny McAfee, you've gotten me into the biggest mess of my entire life!" she exclaimed.

"What did I do?" I demanded, just as angrily.

"If you hadn't blurted out that I could get Cody Tucker for the school dance, none of this would have happened!" Addie shouted.

"Well, if you hadn't been bragging that your dad and Cody were BFFs, then I wouldn't have brought it up at the student council meeting," I said, determined to defend myself.

"I never said they were BFFs," Addie replied. "And besides, if you hadn't been eavesdropping on my conversation with Dana —"

"I wasn't eavesdropping," I interrupted. "*You* were shouting. You *wanted* everyone in the gym to hear it, you show-off."

"What did you call me?" Addie growled.

"A show-off," I repeated. "Because that's what you are."

"At least I have things to show off," Addie shouted back.

I rolled my eyes. "Addie, none of this is going to get Cody Tucker to our formal," I told her.

"No kidding," Addie replied. "*Nothing* is going to get him there. And I'm going to be the laughingstock of the school."

Ordinarily that might have made me happy. After all, Addie had tried to make *me* a laughingstock more than once. But I wasn't happy this time, partly because I really wanted to have Cody Tucker sing at our school dance, and partly because I did feel a little responsible for the mess Addie was in. But *just* a little.

"Maybe we could *hire* Cody Tucker to sing at the dance," I suggested. "We could find out who his manager is and then call and see if he's available. Then we could hold a bake sale or something to get the money to pay for —"

"Are you really that dumb?" Addie shouted at me.

I stared at her. Addie could be pretty mean, but today she was totally out of control. "Excuse me?" I demanded.

"Cody Tucker charges about a million dollars to sing," Addie said.

I frowned. There weren't enough cupcakes in the world to help us raise that kind of money. So much for my plan.

"And what really stinks is that Cody Tucker is right here in town," Addie continued. "He's got meetings at my dad's office all week to go over the tour dates and the promotion schedule. If only I could just talk to him for five minutes, I know I could persuade him."

I stopped for a minute. "Did you say Cody is going to be at your dad's office *this* week?" I asked her.

"Yeah. So what?"

"Then that's the answer! You'll go to your dad's office and ask him!"

Addie looked at me like I'd grown three heads. "And how am I supposed to do that? My dad's office is half an hour away from here. I can't just walk there."

"You can go to work with him on Wednesday," I told her. "It's Bring Your Child to the Office day. Tell him you're really interested in learning about what he does and he'll take you."

Addie couldn't argue with that. She knew as well as I did that parents love when you're interested in what they do.

"And then while you're there you can slip away, find Cody Tucker, and convince him to sing at the dance," I continued.

Addie stared at me for a minute, processing what I'd just told her. Then, finally, she said, "You want me to just walk up to Cody Tucker and ask him if he'll sing at our dance?"

I shrugged. "Do you have a better plan?" I asked.

"No," Addie admitted.

"Good, then it's settled," I said.

"Not quite," she told me.

"Why?" I asked. "It's a perfect plan."

"Not if I get caught sneaking around my dad's office," Addie told me. "I need someone to act as a lookout."

"So ask Dana or Maya to go with you," I suggested.

"I can't do that and you know it," Addie insisted.

She was right. If she invited one of them, she'd have to admit that she'd made up the whole thing about her dad knowing Cody Tucker.

"You'll have to come with me," Addie said flatly.

"Me?" I asked.

"Yes, you," Addie replied. "You're the perfect person. My dad will definitely say yes if I tell him *you* want to come."

That was true. Our parents were so desperate for us to become friends again, they'd do just about anything.

"But, Addie, I don't really think I'm the right person," I said.

"Hey, it's your plan," she reminded me. "And if it wasn't for your blabbing, I wouldn't be in this mess to begin with." She paused for a minute. "Don't you *want* to meet Cody Tucker in person?" she asked me.

Man, she was good. "Yeah, of course," I replied.

"Good. Then it's settled," Addie declared triumphantly.

*   *   *

"Hey, Jenny, wait up," Chloe called out as I closed my locker door and began heading to my first period English class. "I'll walk with you."

I looked over at Chloe curiously. She was wearing a T-shirt with a four-leaf clover on it. She had a pink-and-orange rabbit's foot hanging from the loop of her jeans, a horseshoe necklace around her neck, and a Cody Tucker button pinned to her backpack. It was a weird outfit – even for her.

"What's with the outfit?" I asked her.

"The team has its first wrestling meet after school," she told me. "I want to bring them as much luck as possible."

I laughed. "Oh, I think you will," I assured her. "I get the clover, the horseshoe, and the rabbit's foot, but what about the Cody Tucker button?"

"That one's just for me," Chloe said with a grin. "I gotta keep my Cody close."

I winced slightly at the thought of having Cody close by. "Anyway," I said, changing the subject, "did you have a good weekend?"

"It was okay," she said. "How was yours?"

"Good. I went to the mall and got my outfit for the dance," I told her. "It's a red dress and –"

Before I could finish my sentence, a flashbulb went off in the hall. Marc had just snapped a picture of Chloe. "That's a great candid," he told her. "We'll put it at the beginning of the eighth grade photo section. Underneath we can write, 'Wishing our graduates luck.'"

"Perfect!" Chloe exclaimed happily.

I didn't say anything. I wasn't as into this whole yearbook thing as Chloe and Marc were. I had other things on my mind. Things like having to spend all day Wednesday with Addie Wilson (which was bad), and possibly meeting Cody Tucker (which was very, very good!).

During lunch, Chloe did her very best to talk about the upcoming wrestling meet. Much to her dismay, though, the people at our table were far more interested in discussing the Winter Formal. That should have made me happy. After all, I was the one who had wanted everyone to be excited about it. Unfortunately, I was also the one who knew that Cody Tucker might not be there. In fact, I was the only one, besides Addie, who knew that. And that made it very hard to just sit there listening to my friends go on and on about him.

"Do you guys think Cody Tucker will sing some of his old stuff?" Liza asked. "Because 'Daydreamin'' is one of my favorite songs."

"Mine, too," Marilyn cooed.

"I love when his voice goes up really high on the chorus," Carolyn added.

"I like his new stuff better," Josh said. "It has more of an edge to it."

We all stopped and stared at him for a minute.

"What?" Josh asked. "Guys like Cody Tucker's music, too, you know."

"We know," Liza assured him kindly. "I guess we just didn't think you were the kind of guy who listened to pop music."

I knew exactly what Liza meant. Josh is practically a genius. And he's usually very, very serious. I always figured he was more into Beethoven and Mozart than Cody Tucker.

"Must be Felicia's influence on him," Marc teased.

Josh blushed. He always gets embarrassed when someone jokes about Felicia being his girlfriend, even though she is. It's not that he doesn't like having a girlfriend. He just doesn't like talking about it.

"I was instant messaging with a friend of mine back in London last night," Sam said, changing the subject back to Cody Tucker. "When I told her who was going to be singing at our Winter Formal, she thought I'd gone stark raving mad! Not that I blame her. I mean it is pretty unbelievable."

Yeah it is, I thought wryly. But of course I didn't say that. Addie's secret was safe with me.

Not that Addie was being as considerate of my feelings as I was of hers. In fact, as she and the Pops passed by our table on their daily trip to the girls' room, she was downright mean.

"Did you and your *mommy* have a nice day at the mall?" Claire asked me.

"I'll bet you had to sit in the car seat all the way home," Dana added.

I blushed beet red and looked down at the table. Even though I knew my friends wouldn't care about me going to the mall with my mom, it was still embarrassing. And it didn't help when Addie chimed in. "Jenny, you are such a baby," she said. "I can't believe my parents are making me take you to Bring Your Child to the Office day."

"Addie!" Sabrina exclaimed. "You're bringing *her*?"

"It's not my fault," Addie said. "My dad is forcing me to. You think I want to spend the whole day with Jenny McAfee?"

That did it! I didn't have to take this! I was going to get back at Addie once and for all. I opened my mouth and got ready to shout out that Addie hadn't even been able to get Cody Tucker for our dance, but then I stopped myself. I didn't want to be the one to disappoint my friends. Besides, the plan might work, and Cody might come, and then I'd look like the idiot. So instead I just said, "It wasn't my idea, Addie. I don't exactly want to spend the day with you, either."

The Pops just laughed at that. Obviously they found it really hard to believe that there was someone in the school who didn't want to spend an entire day with Addie Wilson.

"Don't worry, you guys," Addie assured her friends as they walked away. "Even though I can't take any of you with me, I'll bring back lots of Cody Tucker tour buttons for you."

I sighed. Hopefully we'd be bringing back a whole lot more than buttons.

That night, Chloe called me right after dinner. At least I thought it was Chloe. The voice on the other end of the phone was so excited it was hard to tell.

"We won!" the person on the other end shouted. "It was so awesome!"

"Chloe?" I asked.

"Of course it's me, who else would it be?"

That was true. Of all my friends, Chloe was the one who was the most enthusiastic about things. "*Who* won, Chlo?" I asked her.

"The wrestling team," she told me.

"Oh right, the meet was today," I recalled.

"I'll tell you, all of my good luck charms really came in handy. We won big-time!" Chloe exclaimed.

"I never knew you were so superstitious," I said.

"Lots of athletes are superstitious," Chloe replied.

I wouldn't exactly call *managing equipment* for the boys' wrestling team athletic, but Chloe seemed to think it was, so I didn't argue with her.

"I read in a magazine that there are baseball players who are so superstitious they even have lucky under-wear," she continued. "They wear the same pair of underpants for every game until they finally lose. Then the underwear's not considered lucky anymore."

"I hope they wash the underwear in between games," I said.

"They can't do that," Chloe explained. "That would rinse away the luck."

"Okay, that's just gross!" I exclaimed.

Chloe giggled. "Hey, if it works for them, why not?" she said. Then she let out a long, loud yawn. "I am so tired. Taking care of the wrestling team is a lot of work."

"I'm sure it is," I told her. "Why don't you go to bed early tonight?"

"I can't," she replied. "I have lots of homework, and then I have to do some stuff for the Environment Club. I was going to do that in study hall tomorrow, but that's my time to work in the school office."

"Wow, you've got a busy schedule," I said.

"Yeah, but it will all be worth it when I have my picture on almost every page of the yearbook," Chloe told me. "Anyhow, I've gotta go. I want to hang up this lucky T-shirt so it's all aired out for the next meet."

"You're not going to wash the shirt because it might rinse away the luck, right?" I teased.

But Chloe didn't hear the humor in my voice. "Exactly," she agreed. "But I don't think airing it out will do anything bad to it."

I didn't know what to say to that. After all, this was Chloe's superstition, not mine.

"See you tomorrow in school, Chlo."

As I hung up the phone, I thought about asking Chloe if I could borrow that lucky shirt (although, I'd probably wash it first!). I had a feeling that come Wednesday, I was going to need all the luck I could get.

Chapter
SEVEN

AS I GOT INTO Addie's father's car on Wednesday morning, I realized a lucky shirt wasn't what I was going to need at all. A sledgehammer was more like it. You can't use a shirt to break ice. And Addie was definitely being icy toward me.

"Good morning, Jenny," Mr. Wilson said as I sat down in the backseat by myself. Addie was up front next to her dad. She didn't even turn around to say hi or acknowledge that I was there.

"Hi, Mr. Wilson," I answered, trying to sound as upbeat as possible. "Hey, Addie."

She grumbled something and then began fiddling with the stereo.

Mr. Wilson obviously sensed the tension, because he continued making cheery small talk with me. "Addie's in charge of the music today," he said. "That should make you very happy. I'll bet you and Addie like pretty much the same groups."

Actually, I had no idea what music Addie liked to listen to, with the exception of Cody Tucker, that is. And of course, his music was what she put on as we drove.

"Oh, I actually like this song," Mr. Wilson said. Suddenly he began to sing along. But he stopped just as suddenly, probably as a response to an evil stare from Addie. I wasn't sure because, like I said, she was sitting in the front seat and I was in the back. But I knew Addie wouldn't want her dad to sing in front of anyone else. No kid likes that, but it's the kind of thing the Pops, in particular, would be sensitive about.

"Did Addie mention that my company is sponsoring Cody Tucker's tour?" Mr. Wilson asked me.

Mention it? Oh, yeah, big time, I thought to myself. But out loud I just said, "I think she may have said something about it."

"I hear he's a really nice guy," Mr. Wilson said. "The folks in our marketing department are really excited to be working with him. They've been in closed-door meetings all week."

"Are you on the same floor as the marketing department, Dad?" Addie asked him.

I smiled. *Good work, Addie*, I thought. *Find out where Cody's going to be today.*

"No," Mr. Wilson replied. "I'm on nine and marketing's on ten."

"What floor will we be on?" I asked.

"You guys will be on twelve," Mr. Wilson told me. "They have all sorts of fun projects for the kids set up in the conference rooms up there."

I couldn't see her, but I could just imagine Addie rolling her eyes at that. Not that I blamed her. Grown-ups' ideas of fun projects are never quite the same as ours.

We drove on in silence for a while after that. I stared out the window at the passing cars as we made our way into the city. My mind was racing. It was too bad we weren't on the same floor as Cody Tucker. It wasn't going to be easy to sneak down two flights to find him — especially if he was in closed-door meetings with people who worked at Mr. Wilson's company. But somehow we were going to have to find a way to get to him. Our school's Winter Formal depended on it!

Things certainly didn't start out very well. As soon as we arrived at Mr. Wilson's office, Addie and I were dragged off to a meeting room on the twelfth floor of the building. There we were forced to sit through lectures by people who worked at the company — a supervisor from the accounting department who talked about how important math was, a manager from the human resources department who described how to dress when you go on an interview (which I figured I wouldn't be doing for at least ten years!), and a representative from the technology department who explained that the computer system was the most important part of corporate communications. After a while, I realized that even though we'd been sitting there for at least two hours, I still had absolutely no idea what kind of business Mr. Wilson actually worked for. So when Mrs. Draper, the woman in charge of Bring Your Child to the Office day, said we could go for a bathroom break, I thought I was going to scream with relief.

It looked like Addie felt like screaming, too. Only she wanted to scream at me. "Great plan, Jenny," she growled sarcastically. "We're never getting off this floor. We're never going to get a chance to meet Cody Tucker."

I didn't feel any better about things than Addie did. I knew she was right. I sighed heavily and leaned against a wall in the hallway. From the corner of my eye, I spotted a woman pushing a cart with a coffeemaker and some snacks on it. "Are those for us?" I asked Mrs. Draper.

She shook her head. "That's the coffee cart. Fern takes it to every floor so our employees all get a chance to buy snacks or coffee without having to leave the building."

Suddenly I smiled. I knew exactly how we were going to get to Cody Tucker.

"You know, Mrs. Draper, I was hoping to get some real work experience today," I said. "Not working on an account or anything. Just something simple."

"That's very ambitious, um . . ." Mrs. Draper looked down at my name tag. "Jenny. But we don't usually give our visitors jobs."

"Couldn't my friend Addie and I do something simple?" I asked. "Like maybe we could take the coffee cart to her dad's floor? We're very good at arithmetic. We'd have no problem making change."

Mrs. Draper thought for a moment. "That's a very nice idea," she said. "If you two would like to do that, I don't see what harm it would do. Let me just tell Fern to take a break and you two can go down to her father's floor."

"Great!" I exclaimed. As Mrs. Draper went off to talk to Fern, I pulled Addie by the arm. "Come on," I urged.

"Why?" Addie asked. "I don't want to go around selling coffee to people." She sighed heavily. "I can't believe you talked me into this."

"Just trust me, Addie," I whispered. "Follow my lead."

Addie scowled at that. She didn't usually follow anyone. But the expression on my face told her that there was no point in arguing.

"Now you two girls enjoy yourselves," Mrs. Draper said. "And remember to be professionals. This is an office, after all."

"Yes, ma'am," I said. "Thank you for the opportunity."

As Mrs. Draper walked back to the conference room, I pushed the button for the elevator. A moment later it opened. I pushed the cart in, and Addie followed closely behind me. As the doors shut I hit the number 10.

"What are you doing?" she asked. "My dad's on the ninth floor."

"I know," I assured her. "But Cody Tucker is in a meeting on the *tenth* floor."

"Oh," Addie said as my plan became clear to her. "That's pretty smart, Jenny."

I smiled at the compliment. It wasn't often Addie gave me one of those. "Thanks," I said proudly.

"Now, when we find Cody, let me do the talking," Addie said, suddenly taking over as the leader. "I'm much better at talking to celebrities than you are."

"Since when?" I asked. "You've never met any celebrities."

"Neither have you," Addie reminded me. "But I'm a lot better at persuading people to do things than you are."

That was true. Addie could pretty much get anyone to do anything. For example, here I was at her dad's office coming up with a crazy scheme to meet Cody Tucker.

"I'm just more comfortable around everyone," Addie continued. "I don't get all freaked out by people the way you do."

I opened my mouth to defend myself, but then I stopped. I knew she was right. I could be pretty shy around new people. And a new person who was also famous would probably be really intimidating. "You're right," I admitted. "Once we figure out which room Cody Tucker's in, you can take it from there."

Addie smiled triumphantly as the elevator doors opened. But her grin faded as we walked out into the hallway. The tenth floor was just one long series of closed doors. "How are we supposed to figure out which conference room Cody's in?" Addie asked me.

"I guess we have to knock on every one of them," I said.

"Can we do that?" she asked me.

I shrugged. "Why not? We have the coffee cart. I'm sure everyone needs a snack during a meeting."

"That's true," Addie said. She pushed the cart toward the first door. "You knock on it," she said.

"Why me?" I asked. I was suddenly feeling nervous.

"Because I'm going to be doing the talking," Addie said. "Why should I have to do everything? We're in this together, aren't we?"

Not exactly, I thought. *This is really your problem.* But I didn't feel like arguing with Addie. I just wanted to get this over with. So I knocked on the door.

A moment later, I came face-to-face with a rather stern-looking man in a suit and tie. "You're not the usual coffee girl," he said to me.

I gulped and just stared at him. He definitely did not sound nice.

"Fern is taking a break," Addie said sweetly. "We're here representing the Bring Your Child to the Office program."

"Well, make it fast," the man said. "We're in the middle of annual reports here."

I frowned. Annual reports. That meant this wasn't the room Cody Tucker was in. Still, we had a job to do. And the faster we got out of this conference room, the sooner we would find Cody.

Pouring coffee shouldn't be difficult. But with that mean man staring at me, it was hard for me to hold the paper cups still enough. I spilled a drop on the cart, and a little more on the carpet. Addie had to take over, while I collected money and made change.

A few minutes later, we were out of there. "See, Jenny, that's why I have to be the one to talk to Cody about singing at the Winter Formal," Addie said smugly. "You can't even pour coffee around strangers."

I sighed heavily. I was getting really sick of Miss High and Mighty Addie Wilson. "So I spilled a little coffee, big deal," I said finally.

"It would've been a huge deal if you'd spilled it all over Cody Tucker," Addie reminded me. "What if you'd burned him? I read somewhere that he has very delicate skin." We stopped at the next conference room door. "Well?" Addie demanded. "Knock."

I did as I was told. And the minute the door opened, I knew we'd found him. There were posters of Cody Tucker leaning on easels all around the conference room. And the woman who opened the door for us was holding a Cody Tucker button in her hands.

"Oh, good!" the woman said. "The coffee cart is here. You guys want anything?"

"Can y'all just get me some hot water for my throat?"

The minute I heard that slow, southern accent, I knew the person who wanted hot water was Cody Tucker. I'd recognize his voice anywhere.

Addie recognized his voice, too. I could see it in her

eyes. There was a look of excitement — and utter panic — on her face.

"You're not the regular coffee cart girl," the woman said to us.

"Um . . . we're helping out today," I said. "We're here for the Bring Your Child to the Office day thing."

"Oh," the woman said. "I didn't know they were actually *putting* you kids to work today."

I looked over at Addie. She was just standing there, with her hands on the cart. "Come on," I whispered.

But Addie didn't move. It was like she was frozen. So I took the cart and began pushing it into the room. And that's when I saw him. Cody Tucker! Right there in the same room as us!

I glanced over at Addie, hoping she would walk over and say something to him about our Winter Formal. But Addie just stood there, staring at Cody with her mouth wide open.

I knew we only had a few seconds before we would have to get out of there. Addie had to start talking. I glared at her, and then pushed her slightly toward Cody. Addie took a step forward and blurted out, "Cody Tucker! Do you know who you are?"

Everyone in the room started laughing. Especially Cody. "Yeah, I think I do," he said.

For the first time since I had met her, Addie Wilson began to blush. And I mean really blush. Her face turned fire-engine red! Tears began to well up in her eyes.

I knew I had to step in. "Mr. Tucker, sir, um, well, my friend and I have something to ask you."

"Do you want an autograph?" Cody asked me.

"No."

Cody stared at me. "You *don't* want an autograph?" he asked, surprised.

"No, I mean, yes, I would love one," I said. "But that's not what we wanted to ask you. We're not really here because we wanted to deliver coffee on Bring Your Child to the Office day. We came here to ask you if you would sing at our middle school Winter Formal."

The laughter started up again. It was even louder and harder this time. I blushed so red that my cheeks now matched Addie's perfectly.

A chubby, balding man in a gray suit stood up and walked over to me. "Young lady," he said firmly, "Cody Tucker doesn't sing at school dances. He sings in huge arenas. Now why don't you and your friend just take a few buttons and an autograph and get out of here?"

Now I could feel tears forming in *my* eyes. My plan hadn't worked. Our school dance was doomed.

"Now wait, Phil," the woman who'd opened the door for us interrupted. "These girls may be on to something."

"We *are*?" I asked. Then I caught myself. "I mean, we are," I said more confidently, although I had absolutely no idea what exactly we were on to.

"After all, middle school girls are a big part of your fan base," the woman continued. "They *all* dream of having you perform at their school dances."

"So?" Phil asked.

"Think of the publicity an appearance at a school would give Cody," the woman continued. "He's made these kids' dreams come true. He'll be an even bigger hero than ever to the middle school fan base."

"Nicole is right," a man at the far end of the table said. "This could be really good for public relations."

"You want Cody Tucker to put on a free concert?" Phil asked. He did *not* sound pleased.

"Not a whole concert," Nicole replied. "Just one or two songs. He'd be in and out in a few minutes. It would be just long enough for the entertainment shows to shoot a little tape of kids screaming in a middle school gym while he sings."

"Well, actually, our dance is in the cafeteria," I corrected her.

Nicole laughed. "The cafeteria, then," she agreed. She turned to Cody. "Of course, this is all up to you," she told him. "Do you *want* to sing at their dance?"

Cody looked at Addie and me. I tried to give him my brightest, most hopeful smile. Addie was still standing there with her mouth open and her cheeks bright red.

"Sure, why not?" Cody said. "It could be fun. I haven't played a small room in a long time."

I couldn't believe my ears. "You'll do it?" I asked him.

Cody nodded. "Yes."

"We'll have to set up security at the school," Phil told Nicole. "And we'll need permission from the principal, I guess."

"We can get you that, can't we, Addie?" I said.

Addie nodded, but didn't say a word. That was okay, though, because I'd already heard the most important word ever — and it had come straight from Cody Tucker's own lips. The word was *yes*.

Chapter
EIGHT

MY FRIENDS had *lots* of words for me the next morning. Mostly they were filled with excitement.

"You actually met Cody Tucker?" Felicia asked me for about the one hundredth time as we got off the bus together.

I nodded. "He was really nice."

"Did he smile at you?" she asked. "You know, with that half grin?"

I shot her a half grin. "Do you mean this one?"

"That's it," Felicia replied.

"Then, yes," I told her.

Addie walked past us on her way to join her friends. "He was smiling at *me*," Addie insisted. "Don't make it sound like you were the only girl in the room yesterday, Jenny."

It had practically seemed that way to me when we'd been there, the way Addie had just stood there looking stupid. But she'd deny being tongue-tied if I mentioned it, so I didn't bother. Besides, I knew the truth. And so did Cody Tucker.

Word spread like wildfire around the parking lot.

Before long, everyone knew that Addie and I had met Cody Tucker. And everyone wanted details.

"What was he wearing?" Sam asked. "Did he have that single feather dangling from his ear?"

I shook my head. "I don't think so," I told her. "But I really was staring at his eyes more than anything else."

"Oh, wow," Carolyn whispered. "I think I'm going to die."

"Me, too," Marilyn said.

"I'm going to draw a picture of him and give it to him at the dance," Liza said. "It will be a little token of our appreciation for his performance at our dance."

"I know he'd like that," I assured her.

"I guess spending the day with Addie Wilson wasn't so bad," Rachel said.

"I was definitely rewarded for the effort," I told her.

Just then, Chloe came rushing over. I could tell she'd heard the news, because she was wearing yet another new Cody Tucker T-shirt and a big smile.

"You have no idea how jealous I am," she said as she greeted me. "Did you kiss him?"

I looked at her curiously, and laughed, remembering her whole pillow-kissing thing. "No, of course not. It was all about business."

"Well, that's pretty amazing, anyway," she said, before letting out a huge yawn.

"Are we boring you?" Felicia asked Chloe.

Chloe shook her head. "No, I'm sorry," she said. "I'm

just so tired. I was up really late last night finishing homework."

"Did we get a lot?" I asked, suddenly worried about what I had missed in my classes the day before.

"No," Chloe assured me. "It's just that I didn't get home until eight o'clock because of wrestling practice. And I'd wanted to do my English homework during study hall, but I didn't have study hall yesterday. And then, right in the middle of doing my math, I remembered I had e-mails to send out for the Environment Club."

"That's a lot of stuff to do," I told her.

"I know," Chloe said with a sigh. "And I'm going to be completely exhausted after we have our buddy mentoring session with the kindergartners this afternoon. But it will all be worth it when I get my picture in the yearbook on all those pages."

I looked over at Chloe. She had dark circles under her eyes and she kept yawning. She may have thought it was all worth it, but I wasn't so sure.

That afternoon, Sam came over to hang out and work on English homework together. I always like working with Sam on English, because she speaks the real deal, not the American version of English that we speak. I suspect that's why she's Ms. Jaffe's favorite student, too.

"I'm still gobsmacked over the fact that you met Cody Tucker," Sam said as she fed treats to my two pet mice. "And I can't believe he's coming to our school."

"Believe it," I assured her. I smiled. It was good to be able to say that with confidence now.

Sam pushed the last treat into the cage, and then walked over to my bedroom mirror. "How do you think Chloe looked in those pictures the yearbook staff was taking this afternoon?" she asked me. "It's too bad she's not allowed to wear makeup yet. She could've used a little cover-up under her eyes." Sam turned her head slightly and smiled at the mirror. Then she faced front and lifted her chin.

"What are you doing?" I asked her.

"We've got our individual yearbook photo sessions tomorrow," Sam explained. "I'm just trying to figure out the best pose."

"I've never taken a middle school yearbook photo before," I said. "I wonder what you're supposed to wear."

"You can wear pretty much anything you want, according to the letter they sent home last week," Sam replied.

"I know," I said. "But I don't know what to choose."

"We could use some advice," Sam agreed.

"I know where we can get that!" I exclaimed suddenly. Then I leaped off my bed and turned on my computer.

"Let me guess," Sam teased. "Middleschool survival.com."

"Yep," I agreed. "And here's just what we were looking for."

Smile! It's Yearbook Photo Time

They say a picture's worth a thousand words. You want your yearbook photo to tell everyone in school just who you are. It's your signature shot. Here's how to make the most of it.

1. **Try on your outfit before photo day.** You probably already know what colors look best on you, but it doesn't hurt to spend a little extra mirror time making sure that you've picked the best shades for your skin tone. Try to stay away from bold patterns — they can distract from your natural beauty. And leave the bulky sweaters in your closet. Keep it soft and simple. You want people to notice you, not your clothes.

2. **Cover up those zits.** High-fashion models may have the luxury of getting their blemishes airbrushed out of their photos, but yearbook shots are strictly low budget. A little concealer will go a long way toward hiding the pimple that popped up on your chin this morning.

3. **It's all about the angles.** Spend some time looking in the mirror the day before your photo session. Try tilting your face in several directions so you can

figure out what your best angle is. Here are a few hints: Tilt your chin up slightly to avoid the dreaded double chin effect. But if you're wearing your glasses in your photo, tilt your head down slightly to avoid a glare on your lenses.

4. **Stick your neck out.** Turn your head at an angle so just three-quarters of your face is actually facing the camera, and then stick your neck out without actually thrusting out your chin. This gives your bone structure better definition. But be sure to practice this in front of the mirror until you get it just right, as it can be a bit awkward at first.

5. **Chill out.** Many people look weird in their pictures because their features appear frozen. That's what happens when you try too hard to hold a pose until you hear the click of the camera. To avoid that stressed-out, icy look, try taking a deep breath and exhaling slowly. As you let the air out, smile naturally for the camera.

"That helps a lot," Sam said, sticking her neck out slightly as she checked her reflection in the mirror.

"Yeah," I agreed as I went over to my closet and began looking through my shirts for the perfect look. "We're going to look amazing."

"I hope so," Sam said. "Because I don't think that buddy mentoring group picture they took today turned out too great. At least not for me. I'm pretty sure my eyes were shut. And that's the only group shot I'm going to be in. I'm not in other activities the way you are."

"The only other activity I have is student council," I told her. "It's not like I'm Chloe or anything."

"No one's quite like Chloe," Sam said with a giggle.

"That's for sure," I agreed.

"Where's Chloe?" Rachel asked the next morning as the sixth graders lined up for our yearbook photos.

"Maybe she's in the computer lab doing something for the Environment Club," I suggested.

"I'm sure she's not in any hurry to have her picture taken today," Felicia said. "She had three photo sessions yesterday alone."

"I know," I said. "But this is the *individual* shot. You would think she'd be the first one in line for her solo shot."

But Chloe wasn't the first in line—or the last in line, either. In fact, she wasn't in line at all. For a minute, I thought about pulling out my cell phone and giving her a quick call to see where she was. But Ms. Jaffe was standing nearby and we're not supposed to use our cell phones anywhere in the school. And I couldn't sneak into the bathroom to call her, either, because I would lose my place in line.

A few minutes later, I found myself sitting in a chair in front of a photographer. Our school activity photos were all shot by the kids in the yearbook and film clubs, but the portraits were taken by a professional, just like they'd been in elementary school. I smoothed the front of my turquoise-colored shirt (it made my eyes look really green), stuck my neck out (just a little bit), and tilted my chin slightly upward. I'd practiced the pose last night. I took a deep breath and smiled for the camera.

"That's it," the photographer told me after he took my picture. "You looked terrific."

"Thanks," I said. I felt pretty good about myself after that, until I heard him tell Felicia that she looked terrific, too. Then he said the exact same thing to Rachel and Sam. Apparently, that's what he told everyone.

Oh, well. I was just going to have to wait and see how the picture turned out. But I wasn't too worried. Middleschoolsurvival.com had never let me down before. I doubted it would now.

Too bad Chloe couldn't say the same thing for her alarm clock. When I entered the cafeteria at lunchtime, she was already sitting at our table, looking really depressed.

"I can't believe I forgot to set my alarm," Chloe groaned. "I missed the whole morning of school."

"Didn't your mom wake you?" I asked her.

"She said she tried but I wouldn't budge," Chloe explained. "She thought I was sick, so she let me sleep. When I got up and she saw I was okay, she drove me to school. But, of course, by then I'd already missed the yearbook photo sessions."

"So you're not sick?" I asked her.

Chloe shook her head. "I'm just wiped out from all the stuff I've been doing lately."

Wow. Talk about ironic. Here Chloe had been joining all these activities just to get her picture in the yearbook, and those same activities had made her miss the most important shot of all.

"And now instead of having a great picture of me above my name, all anyone is going to see is one of those stupid drawings of a blank head without a face," she groaned angrily.

"There's always the make-up session," I told Chloe.

She sighed. "I know, but if you don't miss the photo because you're sick, they charge extra for the make-up session," she said. "And my mom will never give me the money for that. She'll just tell me it was my responsibility to be at school on the day of the photo if I wanted my picture to be in the yearbook."

"Well, at least your picture is going to be all over the other pages," I reminded her.

"I guess," she agreed. "But it's not the same."

"I know," I told her, trying to sound as understanding as I could. "But remember, this is only sixth grade. You still have two more years to get your portrait in a Joyce Kilmer Middle School yearbook."

"You're right," she agreed. But she still didn't sound too happy.

So I changed the topic. "Did you get a new dress for the dance yet?"

"I haven't had time," Chloe replied. "But I'm definitely getting one this weekend. And I'm going to be sure it's blue, because that's Cody's favorite color. I'm going to make sure he notices me if it's the last thing I do."

I giggled. I had no doubt that Chloe would get him to notice her. When Chloe puts her mind to something, she gets it done. Well, except for her individual yearbook portrait, anyway.

Chapter
NINE

APPARENTLY CHLOE wasn't the only one who knew Cody's favorite color was blue. In fact, there was a whole sea of blue dresses at our Winter Formal. Sky blue dresses, navy blue dresses, electric blue dresses, and royal blue dresses were all you could see for miles. I bet there wasn't a blue dress left anywhere in our mall. I was really glad that my dress was red. It made me stand out.

Not that I needed a dress for people to notice me. Ever since Addie and I had returned from Bring Your Child to the Office day, everyone in the school actually knew who I was. And even though Addie had turned things around and made it seem like *she'd* been the one to convince Cody Tucker and his manager that playing at our school was a great idea, people still thought of *both* of us as celebrities. After all, we were the ones who'd actually met him. And now everyone else was hoping to do the same thing.

"I don't know what I'm supposed to do if he comes over to say hello to me," Chloe admitted to Liza, Sam, and me as we stood on the dance floor, waiting for Cody's arrival. "Is there some sort of manners rule for when you meet a celebrity?"

"I don't know," Liza replied. "I've never met one before. What did you do when *you* met Cody, Jenny?"

"I just tried not to shake or faint," I admitted. "That was hard enough."

"So you didn't curtsy or anything?" Chloe asked.

"Of course she didn't curtsy," Sam said, shaking her head in disbelief. "Who do you think he is? A prince?"

"He's *better* than a prince," Chloe told her. "He's the king of my whole world."

I rolled my eyes. Chloe could be such a drama queen sometimes.

"Did you ever meet one of the princes when you lived in England?" Chloe asked Sam.

"Where would I meet them?" Sam replied. "It's not like we have the same friends, you know."

"I just thought because you lived in London, and they lived in London, that you might have met them," Chloe explained.

Sam shook her head and laughed. "You're a funny bird, Chloe," she told her.

Chloe opened her mouth to reply, but stopped herself when a flood of lights lit up the cafeteria.

"Those are the TV crews!" I shouted excitedly. "He's here!"

A hush came over the cafeteria. It was so quiet, I doubted anyone was even breathing. And then Cody

Tucker appeared in the doorway — the very same doorway I used every day to come into lunch. Amazing.

The screams were deafening as the kids spotted him. I think I saw some of the teachers screaming, too. Not that I blamed them. It was hard not to scream. Cody Tucker has that effect on people.

Cody leaped up on the stage, grinned, and waved at the crowd. That just made everyone scream louder.

"He looks like an angel who floated down from heaven," Chloe shouted to me.

I couldn't disagree with her. When Cody stood there on the stage beneath the sparkly paper snowflakes and stars that hung from the ceiling, he really did look heavenly.

Cody stood there for a minute, waving and smiling, and waiting for his band members to take their places behind him. Then he began to sing. *"It's unbelievable that you and I ever met. An unbelievable moment we'll never forget . . ."*

Talk about moments I would never forget! There was no doubt in my mind that no one at Joyce Kilmer Middle School would ever forget this night. I knew I wouldn't, especially because of what happened next. As Cody Tucker finished his first song, he looked out at the crowd and announced, "That was my first single, 'Unbelievable.' Now I'm going to sing a new song for you. It's from my latest CD, and it goes out to the two very special girls who helped bring me to your school. Jenny and Addie, this one's for you."

I stood there for a minute, in shock. Was it possible? Had Cody Tucker just dedicated a song to me? *Me?*

Apparently he had, because my friends were jumping and screaming excitedly all around me.

"Oh my goodness, Jenny!" Chloe squealed. "He said your name. *Your* name passed through Cody Tucker's lips!"

"That was incredible," Liza said.

"I'm blown away!" Sam agreed.

Felicia, Josh, Marc, Rachel, and the twins came running over from where they'd been standing. I understood why they wanted to be with us now. This was an incredible moment, and my friends wanted to be there with me – just the way we'd all been there to cheer Rachel and Felicia on at the basketball championships or to give Chloe a standing ovation at the end of the school musical. My friends and I are there for each other whether things are good or bad. Tonight was *definitely* one of the good times.

Just then, Zoë Leonard, an eighth grader from the yearbook club, came racing over, her camera in her hands. "Jenny, let me get a picture of you and your friends at the Winter Formal. We have to get a picture of you. After all, you're the reason Cody is here. Well, you and Addie Wilson, of course."

"Of course," Chloe said, rolling her eyes. Then she shook her head. "No, tonight I am not going to be anti-Addie. I'm not going to be anti-anything. Cody Tucker is here and all is right with the world."

I smiled as my friends gathered around me for our photos. Chloe was right. Tonight, life at Joyce Kilmer Middle School was absolutely perfect.

The Matter of Manners

Do you know the magic words? No, not abracadabra. The real magic words are *please* and *thank you*. You'd be surprised how many doors they'll open for you. Do you know the proper etiquette for any situation? *Please* take the quiz and find out.

1. When is it okay to eat with your hands at a dinner party?

A. When they're clean.
B. When the table has been set without utensils.
C. If the host tells you to.

2. You're walking down the hallway at school and you bump into someone accidentally. What do you say?

A. Excuse me.
B. Oops.
C. Watch where you're going!

3. When you're finished eating, where do you put your utensils?

A. Under your napkin.

B. On the table.

C. Sideways across your plate.

4. You're invited to a birthday party. The invitation asks you to RSVP no later than one week before the party. What is the most polite thing to do?

A. Don't bother with an RSVP, because you're not sure if you'll feel like going on the day of the party. If you wake up that morning and feel like it, just show up.

B. Call at least a week in advance to let the host know whether or not you will be going.

C. Wait until a day or two before the party to RSVP just in case a better invitation comes.

5. What is the first thing you should do when you sit down at the dinner table?

A. Greet everyone.

B. Drink from your water glass.

C. Put your napkin on your lap.

6. **You are at the mall with your grandmother when you run into two kids you know from your math class. What do you do?**

   A. Introduce the girls to Grandma and try to include her in the conversation.
   B. Talk to the girls and leave your grandmother standing uncomfortably nearby.
   C. Talk to the girls for a few minutes and then say, "Oh, yeah. This is my grandmother."

7. **You're hurrying to the movie theater in the hopes of buying tickets before the show is sold out. As you reach the door, you notice an older man moving slowly a few paces behind you. What do you do?**

   A. Walk faster so you don't have to hold the door for him.
   B. Hold the door and wait patiently for him to go in before you.
   C. Hold the door for him, while rolling your eyes and sighing — just to make sure he knows you didn't have to do this but you are.

8. You and your friends are at the movies. You have dutifully set your phone to "silent," but you feel it vibrate with a text message. What's your reaction?

A. Call the person back and answer — in a whisper, of course. After all, you're in a movie theater.

B. Pull the phone out of your bag and text back. They said the phone had to be silent, not off.

C. Go out into the lobby to make sure the text is not an emergency.

The correct answers are:

1. B
2. A
3. C
4. B
5. C
6. A
7. B
8. C

So, what does your score say about your etiquette know-how?

6–8 correct answers: Congratulations, Miss Manners. You know how to behave well in any situation. No one will ever catch you without your napkin on your lap.

4–5 correct answers: You have some idea of how to behave with class, but every now and then, you slip up a bit. Have you considered picking up a book on etiquette and brushing up on your manners? Knowing what's expected could help give you confidence if you find yourself in a new social situation.

1–3 correct answers: Excuse *you*! Actually, there's no excuse for not knowing even the most basic rules of etiquette. It's a matter of showing the people around you respect. So the next time you're wondering how to behave, just ask yourself a simple question: "How would I want these people to treat me?" Use some good manners and you just might find yourself with a whole bunch of new friends.

Here's a sneak peek at Jenny's next middle school adventure!

As soon as the bus pulled up to my stop, I hurried off and raced the two blocks to my house. Then I burst through the front door.

"I'm home, Mom!" I shouted. "Where's the surprise?"

"We're in the kitchen!" my mother called back.

I zoomed through the living room straight to the

kitchen. And there, sitting in the seat my dad usually sits in, was my surprise.

"Aunt Amy!" I exclaimed. Then I ran over and gave her a huge hug.

"Hi to you too," my aunt laughed.

"I can't believe you're here!" I squealed joyfully.

"I have some time off, so I figured I'd come visit my favorite niece."

I laughed. "I'm your *only* niece," I reminded her.

"Even if your mom had a dozen kids, you'd still be my favorite," Aunt Amy assured me.

I smiled. Aunt Amy always knew exactly the right thing to say. She was incredible and really fun to be around. She was one of the most exciting people I knew, which is why I was kind of surprised she was in my hometown. Life around here isn't exactly exciting.

"I'm flying off to China on business a week from Saturday, and I thought I could use a few quiet, restful days here with you guys first," Aunt Amy said. "I wanted a chance to hang out with you and your mice."

I grinned. Most adults hated my two pet white mice. Even my mom wasn't exactly crazy about them. But Aunt Amy *liked* mice. In fact, she was always saying that one day she was going to create a whole line of greeting cards with pictures of them on the front.

That's what my aunt does. She's the art director for the Connections Greeting Card Company. She flies all over the world, meeting artists and checking on the factories where the cards are manufactured. That was probably why she was flying to China — a lot of the company's greeting cards are printed overseas. My Aunt Amy definitely has a very exciting career.

Career! Suddenly, I smiled broadly. Now I was doubly glad Aunt Amy had arrived. "Are you still going to be in town on Tuesday?" I asked her.

Aunt Amy took a sip of her coffee and nodded. "Mm-hmm. My flight's not until a week from Saturday."

"Great!" I exclaimed.

"Why?" Aunt Amy asked.

"Well, Career Day at my school is on Tuesday, and since I'm on the student council I have to bring someone," I explained. "Aunt Amy, your job is *really* interesting. And since you're on vacation, you won't have to ask your boss for a day off so you can come."

"That's true," Aunt Amy said. "I'm free as a bird."

"Then you'll do it?" I asked her.

"Definitely," Aunt Amy said with a grin. "Anything for my Jennifer Juniper."

I smiled at my favorite aunt's nickname for me. Then I said, "Aunt Amy, can I ask you one more favor?"

"What?"

"Please don't call me that at school."

Aunt Amy chuckled. "No problem — *Jenny*."

Will Jenny survive middle school?
Read these books to find out!

#1 Can You Get an F in Lunch?
Jenny's best friend, Addie, dumps her
on the first day of middle school.

#2 Madame President
Jenny and Addie both run for
class president. Who will win?

#3 I Heard a Rumor
The school gossip columnist
is revealing everyone's secrets!

#4 The New Girl
There's a new girl in school!
Will she be a Pop or not?

#5 Cheat Sheet
Could one of Jenny's friends
be a cheater?

#6 P.S. I Really Like You
Jenny has a secret admirer!
Who could it be?

#7 Who's Got Spirit?

It's Spirit Week! Who has the most school pride – Jenny's friends or the Pops?

#8 It's All Downhill From Here

Jenny has to spend her snow day with her ex-BFF, Addie!

#9 Caught in the Web

Jenny and her friends start a webcast, and so do the Pops! Which show will have more viewers?

#10 Into the Woods

The sixth grade goes to science camp and Jenny, Sam, and Chloe have to share a cabin with the Pops!

#11 Wish Upon a Star

Can Jenny work with Addie to save the winter dance?

#12 I Thought We Were Friends!

Uh-oh! Jenny's feeling jealous of her friend Liza! Can the girls stay friends?